BETRAYED BY
HELL
ERIN BEDFORD

Also By Erin Bedford

<u>The Underground Series</u>
Chasing Rabbits
Chasing Cats
Chasing Princes
Chasing Shadows
Chasing Hearts

<u>The Crimes of Alice</u>
The Crimes of Alice
Hatter's Heart
Cheshire's Smile

<u>The Mary Wiles Chronicles</u>
Marked by Hell
Bound by Hell
Deceived by Hell
Tempted by Hell
Betrayed By Hell

<u>Starcrossed Dragons</u>
Riding Lightning
Grinding Frost
Swallowing Fire
Pounding Earth

<u>Curse of the Fairy Tales</u>
Rapunzel Untamed
Rapunzel Unveiled
Rapunzel Unchained

<u>Her Angels</u>
Heaven's Embrace
Heaven's A Beach
Heaven's Most Wanted

<u>House of Durand</u>
Indebted to the Vampires
Wanted by the Vampires
Protected by the Vampires
Embrace of the Vampires
Tempted by the Butler
Loved by the Vampires
Huntress of the Vampires
Judged by the Vampires
Imprisoned by the Vampires

<u>Academy of Witches</u>
Witching On A Star
As You Witch
Witch You Were Here
Just Witch It
Summer Witchin'

<u>Children of the Fallen</u>
Death In Her Eyes
Fire In Her Blood

<u>House of Van Helsing</u>
Her Cross To Bear
Blood Betrayal

<u>The Beast of the Fae Court</u>
<u>Granting Her Wish</u>
<u>Vampire CEO</u>

Dedication

To my fans who have been with me since the first book. It took a few years but we finally finished Mary's adventure!

1

Muriel.

Muriel.

MURIEL!

"Shut up," I muttered and shifted away from the voice. It didn't help. The voice persisted.

Muriel.

"Leave me alone." I lifted my head and grabbed the closest thing to me, throwing it at the voice.

"Ouch, shit, Mary!"

I jerked up all the way, my eyes blinking at the light. "Huh, what?" My gaze swung around the room and seeing the familiar walls of my office/bedroom as I searched for the familiar voice. "Trish?"

"Yeah, you jerk." My black-haired secretary rubbed her head as she bent to pick up the wireless mouse I'd thrown at her. She'd streaked her hair blue today, probably to match the blue stripes of her long-sleeved shirtdress, several heavily decorated black belts overlapping at the waist.

A shirtdress. Really? Either wear a shirt or wear a dress. Why does it have to be both?

"Sorry," I grumbled and pushed back from my chair and the desk. The side of my face was stiff and sore from lying on it all night, and I had a weird, metallic taste in my mouth.

"Are you alright?" Trisha asked, bringing my mouse back over to the desk, her platform heeled black boots louder than an elephant stampede on the dingy hard wood floors. "I was calling your name for a good five minutes and barely got anything out of you."

I leaned over in my chair and rubbed a hand over my face, groaning. "Yeah. Just not sleeping well latcly."

Trisha leaned against my desk, grinning mischievously. "Oooh, late nights with your demon boyfriend?"

Lifting my head, I stared at her incredulously. "Really? Sid, is only half demon and sadly, no." I pushed up out of my chair and practically raced for the coffee pot. I had to get this taste out of my mouth.

"So, what was it? Demon fighting? Research?" Trisha slid into my chair and clacked away on my keyboard. "Please tell me you finally started binge-watching that demon hunter series I told you about."

My cup in my hand, I noticed my nails were caked with dirt. How'd that happen?

Returning my attention to Trisha, I glanced at her over my cup of coffee. I let the bitter liquid sweep over my tongue as I thought of what I was going to tell her. In all honesty, last night was a blur. I wasn't exactly sure what I did. I just knew that I was completely exhausted and felt like I hadn't slept a wink. Not wanting to worry Trisha, I sidestepped the question.

"I'm not going to watch some show about demon hunting when I do it in real life. That's like a doctor watching a sitcom about being a doctor." I strode across the room and reached for a shirt off the office floor. Holding it up to my nose, I sniffed it before shrugging and setting my coffee cup down.

While I exchanged one shirt for the other, Trisha kept at it. "Come on, it's not even about the demon hunting. It's about two brothers as they bond over fighting evil and saving the world. Doesn't hurt that they are hot as hell too."

I shot her a look.

Trisha grimaced. "Sorry, I know hell is kind of a touchy subject . . ." She paused for a moment, pulling her lip between her teeth.

I sat on the end of my pullout bed and changed my socks. "Spit it out already. I know you have something else to say."

Swiveling the chair around to face me, Trisha laced her hands between her legs and leaned forward. "I was going to say, speaking of hell, have you had a chance to get rid of . . ." she wagged her hand around her head.

I frowned. "What?"

"You know . . ." She lowered her voice and whispered quickly, ". . . the demon inside you."

I rolled my eyes. "Trisha, whispering isn't going to keep him from hearing you, and no, I haven't. We have to find him a body to go to first, and that hasn't exactly been a high priority at the moment."

Trisha watched me, not completely convinced. "So you haven't had any issues with him?"

My hands stopped mid-tie of my shoes as I really thought about her question. Todd or Zee, as he told me to refer to him, hadn't really shown up in the last few days. Not since we had that showdown in Madam Serena's shop downstairs. I mean, I guess I wouldn't either. I did put a gun to my head and threaten to take us both out.

Working on my shoes again, I shrugged. "No, not really. He's been pretty quiet for the most part."

Trisha's brow furrowed, bunching up her heavy eye makeup. "Doesn't that worry you?"

I pushed up on my knees to stand and walked back over to my desk. "No, not really." I opened the drawer I usually kept my gun in and frowned. It wasn't there. Glancing around the room, I found it hanging on the coat rack with my jacket. As I moved toward it, I continued, "If he's content just hanging in the background, I'm not going to complain and neither should you." I gave her a stern look as I adjusted my shoulder holster. "I mean it. Leave it alone, Trish."

Trisha made a popping sound with her mouth and sighed, sinking back into her chair. "Fine. I'll drop it . . ." she pointed a finger at me and added on, "for now. But you can't just live with a demon inside of you all the time. I mean, that's got to be messing up your angelic mojo, you know?"

Shrugging on my jacket, I shook my head. "I think out of the two of us, I'm the bigger expert on what will mess up my 'mojo.' And I feel fine. Really. Now, I'm going to go check on my *half* demon boyfriend and see about getting paid from the police for all those jobs we've done for them."

Trisha narrowed her eyes at me. "You actually care about getting paid?"

My hand on the office doorknob, I said, "Well, yeah. How else are we going to renovate Madame Serena's shop? It does require money."

"Yeah, it does," Trisha answered, her eyes boring into my back as I walked away.

I didn't know what her problem was. It wasn't so out of the ordinary for me to worry about money. In heaven, we didn't have to pay for things. It was share and share alike. You got assigned a job, and you did it. When you needed something, you went and got it.

However, this was the human world, and you needed money to survive. Everything cost, and no one was going to give you a free handout. It was about time I got paid for my services.

With Sid back, he was driving his truck again, and that meant I had to go back to driving the old beater that I'd acquired a while ago. At least I didn't have to worry about damaging it on the job. It already had enough damage to it; any more would just be adding character.

My stomach gurgled as I jumped on the interstate to head to Sid's bar. While my body was hungry for food, the very thought of it made me want to vomit. For the second time in a short time, I wondered what happened last night. Had I drunk too much?

I vaguely remembered going out to do some recon on Asmodeus and Lucifer. I needed to know what they were planning now that I had taken Michael's blade and Sid back. They couldn't use him anymore to make me open a portal to heaven. That didn't mean they wouldn't keep trying. As far as I was concerned, there was a target on my back and that of anyone I cared about.

After beating up a few demons for information, I didn't remember if I'd exorcised them or if I'd just left them there. I knew I hadn't gotten much out of them. Nobody wanted to piss off the big guys, and apparently, I wasn't enough of a threat to make them talk.

Unfortunately, the more I tried to remember last night, the cloudier it became.

Which didn't bode well for anyone. Sighing, I pulled off the downtown exit.

Sid's bar, the Night Owl, was a common hangout for the supernatural. Mostly demons, sometimes vampires and other beings, but every once in a while, humans would wander in, and then things got really interesting. I didn't expect much to be happening at ten in the morning, especially since I was able to find a parking spot right up front.

I parked and climbed out of the car, not bothering to lock the thing. Personally, it would be a blessing to have the thing stolen. However, sitting next to Sid's expensive truck, I think it was way down on the list of desirables.

The sign above the bar was off, but I knew Sid would be there anyway. He lived and breathed the bar, and if I ever wondered where he was, it would always be here.

The windows of the bar were tinted to hide what happened on the inside from prying eyes. Once I thought it was to hide demon activity but now I knew it was because Sid used his clientele to feed the incubus inside of him. No one wanted to be watched practically dry humping on the dance floor.

The door to the bar opened easily even with the closed sign on. I walked into the dimly lit room, the dark wood floor and bar making it even more ominous as I searched for my boyfriend.

I didn't have long to search.

Sid's voice called out from the office, "We're closed. Come back later."

I tucked my hands in the pockets of my jeans and sauntered through the empty dance floor, the silence in the place a bit morbid for my taste. I very rarely came outside of hours, and I wasn't sure I liked the place so quiet.

I barely made it across the dance floor before Sid came barreling out of the back room. His forest green shirt pulled against the expansion of his chest, showing off the muscle deliciousness that I knew laid beneath. The shirt was wrinkled as well as the dark jeans he wore fitted tight enough that you couldn't cop a feel if you wanted to. Believe me, I've tried.

It was strange what having sex on the regular would do to one's libido. Things I had once thought were strange and unusual to be obsessed with now made my blood heat and my body ache. For instance, the first time I'd seen Sid in a pair of grey sweatpants. Before having intercourse, I wouldn't have thought anything of them. Now when Sid wore them, my brain seemed to decide all neurons were needed elsewhere. Particularly, low between my thighs.

"I said we're closed . . . oh, it's you." He stopped in his tracks and stared at me.

I arched a brow. "Well, hello to you too."

Sid's lips ticked up in an apologetic smile. "Sorry, I'm a bit cranky when I haven't eaten."

Continuing my walk across the dance floor, I cocked my head to the side as I stopped in front of him. "Eaten as in eaten or as in *eaten?*"

Sid's hazel gaze dipped down, his hands coming up to cup the back of my elbows. "Both." When he looked up at me this time, the hazel of his eyes had darkened, his demon half peeking from beneath the surface.

Licking my lips, I shrugged out of my jacket and laid it on the top of the bar. "Well, I can help with one . . . however the other—"

"I'll cook something after." Sid picked me up by the back of my thighs and sat me on the bar. Pushing between them, he wasted no time pressing his mouth to mine. A rush of need swept through me as Sid let his demon half loose to feed. It caused me to shudder and groan into his mouth, thrusting my hips closer to him.

A year ago, Sid's powers wouldn't have affected me, but the longer I stayed on Earth and the longer I was without my wings, the more human I became. Now Sid's powers were hard to resist. Not that I wanted to. Things between Sid and me were always fire, and with his powers added to the mix, they were molten lava.

"Take your pants off," I commanded, unbuttoning my own.

Sid let out a feral growl as he did what I asked, his eyes watching my hands. I braced my feet on two of the bar stools and lifted my hips, unable to shove my pants off fast enough. Once they were gone, Sid was there, sinking his hot, thick length inside of me.

Every inch of me tightened in anticipation. Sid took his sweet, sweet time, giving me a moment to feel every agonizingly delicious inch of him. My eyes rolled up. My nails dug into the flesh of his arms. "Fuuuuck."

"I thought that was what I was doing," Sid grunted in response, his grip on my thighs almost bruising. The rosary around his wrist bumped against me, leaving cold spots on my skin.

Not thinking about what I was doing, I grabbed a hold of the rosary and jerked as hard as I could, snapping the string and sending beads scattering across the bar and floor.

Sid stared down at what I'd done, his eyes wide. "Mary, what the—" I grabbed both sides of his face and stared into his eyes before shoving him completely inside of me. I thrust my hips, doing most of the work while I watched that darkness behind his gaze push forth. A low growl rumbled from his throat, and then he took over, that growl turning in to a roar. His thrusts were hard and unforgiving, pushing so far inside of me that I knew I would be bruised later.

I didn't care.

I curled my fingers into his hair and pulled on it. "Now you're fucking me."

The sinister smile on Sid's face should have scared me, but it only spurred me on more. Sid jerked out of me and spun me around. Pinned face first against the bar, I couldn't do anything other than let Sid have his way with me. This position gave him a deeper and sharper angle, making me cry out, torn between the pain and pleasure of it.

Sid grabbed a hand full of my hair and pulled on it, forcing my head into an awkward angle as he hissed into my ear. "Is this what you wanted, angel whore?"

I moaned in response.

"Admit it, you've always wanted good boy Sid to let loose on you like this." He licked the side of my face and slapped a hand between my thighs, making me cry out. "You're a slut for demons. That's why you chased your boss out of heaven. It's why you'll never make it back there. Because you want it—this—too fucking bad."

Stars burst behind my eyes as he slammed into me a few more times. Honestly, I lost count. I was too busy riding the wave of whatever the hell just happened. I blacked out for a moment, and the next thing I knew, I was on the bar floor, a towel draped over my privates.

Inching up, I groaned at the ache in my body. Every inch of me hurt, but in a good way. Like when your body ached from a good hard work out. Painful, but satisfying.

I blinked a few times, searching around for Sid. I didn't see him. More than a bit confused, I sat up and found my pants. I used the towel to clean up the mess between my legs, a mixture of fluids and blood. I guess we got a little carried away.

Fully dressed, I grabbed my jacket and walked to the back room. Sid sat in the corner of the room, his head down and his hands cupped in front of him, a different rosary wrapped around his wrist.

"Hey, there you are." I stopped by his desk and peered down at him. "What're you doing?"

Sid lifted his head, anger pinching the skin around his eyes. "What am I doing? What am I doing, Mary?" He jumped out of his seat. "I'm wondering how I almost killed you!"

"Whoa." I held my hands up and backed away from him. "Calm down. You didn't kill me. I'm fine. See?" I held my hands out to my sides and did a little spin. "I'm not human, Sid. You can't kill me from a little rough sex."

"Neither am I. Which you seemed to have forgotten." His fingers curled around the rosary so tight, his knuckles went white. "Why did you even do it? What made you think that was okay?"

I opened my mouth to answer him, but the words caught in my throat. Why had I done it? It wasn't like I hadn't dealt with demon Sid before. But I'd never purposely drawn him out like this.

"Well?" Sid probed, waiting for my answer.

I clamped my mouth shut and shook my head. "I don't know. I wasn't thinking."

"That's right," Sid interrupted me. "You weren't thinking."

I blew out a breath and stepped toward him, my hands outstretched. "Sid."

"Don't." Sid held a hand up and backed away from me. Almost like he was afraid of me touching him.

I stopped and dropped my hands. "Sid, I'm sorry. I don't know what came over me." When he didn't respond, I shifted away. "I'm just gonna . . . I'm just gonna go."

I never left a place so fast in my long life.

What exactly happened in there? Was this a side effect of becoming human? That I would have these unstoppable impulses? If so, then I wasn't sure I wanted them. I'd not only released a demon on purpose, but I did it at the cost of someone I loved most.

What the hell was happening to me? I did know where to go to get answers, though.

THE TREPIDATION IN MY heart lifted as I pulled into the U-shaped drive of the Phoenix Guild, the headquarters of the notorious supernatural hunters, where a large white mansion sat, its tall columns more like a way to look down on the world than to lift it up.

My *other* best friend, Adara, normally lived in an apartment on the other side of town, as far away as she could get from the guild. However, since her father got sick, she had stepped up and taken over the reins. I didn't always agree with the Phoenix Guild's methods. They were too "shoot first and ask questions later" for me. I had to admit, it was handy to have their resources at my beck and call.

I climbed out of my car and stalked up the stairs. Usually, the doors would open before I even hit the front step. This time, I had to open the door myself. Once I stepped inside the building, I realized why.

The place was in an uproar. Hunters rushed from one side of the room to the other, grabbing gear from the hidden walls in the foyer. Several guild members were shouting orders to the others.

"Get that pulled tight. This is not a drill."

"Every minute you waste is a dead body on your conscience. Now pick up the pace."

No one even noticed me standing there at the front door.

Perplexed by the sudden onslaught of activity in the usually poised and secretive place, I carefully made my way through the display cases spread out through the main room. Once upon a time, Trisha and I had snuck into the place to hide the very dagger

I had safely tucked away. Now, the items in the display cases weren't my main objective. The office on the other side of them was.

Two muscular men, dressed all in black and more weapons than seemed necessary for guarding a door, stopped me before I could enter Adara's office.

"Do you have an appointment?" the first one asked, a man with a crew cut and a nose that had been broken so many times that it was permanently pointed off to the side. Crew cut crossed his arms over his chest and visibly straightening to tower over me.

If he was trying to intimidate me, he was doing a piss-poor job. I took on demons for a living. No human with a tiny bit of magic was going to make me back down.

"No," I flatly stated, staring him down.

"No one gets in to see the leader without an appointment." Crew cut tried to dismiss me.

"Leader, huh?" I arched a brow. "That's what you're calling her now?" I smirked and cocked my head to the side, "Because as Adara tells it, you call her a vampire-fucking whore. Or is that only behind her back when she's not signing your paychecks?"

The second of the guards visibly tensed. Crew cut's face grew red, and the veins in his neck bulged. I prepared myself for an attack, verbal or if he was stupid, physical.

The door opened behind them, and Adara's dark head popped out. Her almond shaped eyes flicked to the two guards and then to me. "I thought I heard you out here. Come on." She grabbed me by the arm and tried to jerk me inside. Crew cut latched onto my other arm and resisted.

"Alec said you were not to be disturbed."

Adara's gaze narrowed, and her other hand came up, the palm turning red underneath the skin as if waiting to boil over. "Alec is not my *fucking* boss. I am, and also yours. So I suggest you let go of my friend before I have I make Trevor here, go get an ash tray for your body."

For a second, the guard seemed to think about it. He glared at me and then glanced over to his partner, Trevor I assumed, who shook his head. That seemed to be enough of a reason for him to let me go.

I waited until Adara slammed the door in his face before rubbing my arm where he had grabbed me. The guy had quite a grip on him.

Walking around her office, or what was her father's office before, I notice a few differences. The walls were still covered in shelves of books but there was a television mounted on the wall behind her and several vases of flowers brightening up the place.

"So… you want to tell me what's with the Armageddon that is going on out there?" I threw myself into the chair across from her desk. "It's worse out there than those blow-out sales Trisha makes me go to." I shuddered at the thought of facing down those hordes of angry women willing to kill for a good deal. Give me a demon horde any day versus those crazies.

Adara sighed and clicked a few keys on her laptop before turning it around to face me. The screen showed a chart of the world map with different colors ranging from green, yellow, orange, and red. "We've had a recent rise in demon activity that's ranging all over the place. All the chapters of the Phoenix Guild are on high alert." She pointed at LA, which was covered in a dark red dot. "As you can see, we have an abnormally high amount compared to everywhere else."

I snorted, tapping my foot against the leg of the chair. "That's not surprising."

"That's not the worrying part. While we expected some kind of backlash for taking Sid and the dagger back, this seems a bit extreme. I mean, how are they even getting here this easily?" Turning the laptop back around, Adara clicked a few more buttons before flipping it back to me.

The pictures on the screen were clearly taken at night, the flash on the camera not keeping the shadows in the corners at bay. Corpses—for that's all they could be called now—were ripped into pieces, the parts lined up precariously.

"It's not even just regular old possessions and boring mayhem either. This is violence for the sake of it. Like they are trying to get our attention." She flicked to another picture where the bodies had been cut up but not ripped apart.

Something prodded at the back of my mind. Something familiar about what I was seeing. I couldn't put my finger on it though. I blinked and rubbed a hand over my face. "Do you have any leads?"

Snapping the laptop closed, Adara shook her head. "That's the thing. We've exorcised demons and staked vamps until our throats and fingers bled but these fuckers keep coming up." Swiveling in her chair, she seemed to have a thought. "Do you think they're looking for Michael's blade?"

I shrugged a shoulder. "I don't know. Wouldn't be surprised but then wouldn't they come for me? Not make this big of a mess?"

"Hmmm, possibly. Where is the dagger anyway?"

Clicking my tongue, I met her gaze. "You'll have to ask Trisha that. I have no idea.'

Adara's held tilted slightly. "Don't trust yourself?"

"Don't trust Zee."

Adara bobbed her head in understanding.

"You have to find the ringleader," I pointed out returning to our prior conversation. I let my eyes focus on the pretty yellow flowers in the corner as I talked.

The petals had already begun to droop and shrivel. "They're the ones calling the shots and probably the one getting them here."

"That was my thought exactly." Adara stood from her seat and slapped her hands on her desk, leaning toward me. "That's where you come in."

I frowned, shifting in my seat. "What can I do that you aren't already?"

"Poke around, ask the sergeant or Sid to grill their contacts."

I flinched at the mention of Sid. I hoped Adara hadn't noticed, but she was worse than Trisha when it came to latching onto tells.

"What is it?" Adara rounded the desk and sat on the edge across from me, her long legs crossing at the ankles. The black-on-black outfit seeming to be a fashion statement around here. "What have you done now?"

I scoffed, rocking back in my seat. "Why do you think it's something I did?"

Adara gave me a flat look. "Because you're a freaking angel stuck on Earth. If anyone would mess up things with a tasty morsel like Sid then it would be you."

Sighing, I leaned forward so my hands hung between my legs, trying to figure out how to explain to her what happened. I didn't know why I was so hesitant. Out of the two of us, Adara had done far sketchier things sexually than I would ever know. Believe me, I didn't want to know. No matter how much she tried to tell me.

"Man, must be bad if you're having this hard of a time telling me." Adara pushed off the desk and went to the wall of books. Her back turned to me, Adara removed a few and opened a secret panel that contained a bottle of amber liquid. Turning back to me with a grin, she held the bottle out. "How about a drink and then you can tell Mama Adara all about it?"

I pursed my lips, rolling my eyes. "I don't need to drink to tell you what happened."

Adara handed me a glass anyway and clinked her own against it. "Then just think of it as keeping me company so I can drink."

I stared down at the liquid in my glass and then back to Adara. "Why do you need a reason to drink this early in the day?"

"Uh-uh," Adara shook her head. "We're talking about you, not me."

"Fine, but we're rounding back to you," I pointed out before throwing back the entire contents of my glass. I grimaced and set the glass on the table slightly harder than intended.

"Whoa, and I thought I needed the drink," Adara murmured, sipping from her glass her swiveling from side to side.

Ignoring her comment, I stared at the empty glass. "Have you ever done something so out of character, you didn't even know you did it until you had already done it?" I pressed my lips together firmly and then wiped my hands on my pants, the dampness on them a new sensation for me. "That doesn't even make sense to me saying it out loud."

Adara studied me in silence and then commanded, "Tell me what happened."

I explained how things had gone down with Sid. I told her every nitty-gritty naked detail. When I was done, I looked to my friend. Usually, Adara would have been giddy over the chance to hear about my sexual encounters, but the unreadable expression on her face worried me.

"Normally, in this kind of situation, I would chalk it up to being in the moment." Adara brought her glass up to her lips once more, taking a few seconds to gather her thoughts. When she sat it back down, the hardened look in her eyes made me flinch. "However, with that demon still inside of you, anything is possible. How are things with your little parasite?"

I shrugged, crossing one leg over the other and lacing my hands in my lap. "Quiet. Hasn't said a word since I threatened to blow both our heads off."

Adara gaped at me. Clamping her mouth shut as she recovered, she waved me off. "Suicidal tendencies aside, the silence is concerning. Could he be taking control of you?"

I shifted in my seat again, contemplating her words. "No, no way. I'd know if I was being controlled. I'm an archangel. You think some lowly demon is going to get the best of me?" I scoffed and gestured wildly. "I might not have all of my celestial powers, but I think that I have enough to keep control of my own mind and body."

"Hey, hey." Adara lifted her hands in front of her. "No need to get upset. I was just suggesting it. Though, if it's not that . . ." She trailed off and looked to the side. "Then perhaps your celestial aura is overpowering his? He may not have the strength to talk to you anymore."

"You think so?" I scooched onto the edge of my seat, a bit more eager than I should have been at someone's demise.

Adara shrugged. "Who knows. Stranger things have happened. And hey, if it's true, it means you don't have to live up to your side of the deal and give it some poor human as a meat suit for it to pilot."

"That sounds good to me." I paused for a moment and then added on, "What do you say, Zee?"

Silence.

"Zee?" Adara prompted. "I thought his name was Todd."

I shook my head. "I think that was his human name. Zee is probably his demonic name. However, he's still not answering. So

I'm going with your theory." I clapped my hands together and stood. "Well, that makes me feel better . . . and worse." I sank back into my chair. "If it's not the demon making me act out of character, that means I did that to Sid all on my own."

Adara gave me a sympathetic smile. "Sorry, kid. Them's the breaks. Sometimes we do fucked-up shit to the ones we love. Just give him time. Then you guys can talk it out, and it will be all hunky-dory."

"But what if it isn't?"

"Then," Adara opened her laptop once more, turning her gaze away from me, "it isn't."

"That's not comforting," I shot back.

Lifting a shoulder and dropping it, Adara clicked away on her keyboard. "Hey, you came to someone whose only love of her life was killed by her own father. What kind of advice did you expect?"

"Alright, alright. I get it. I'm on my own with this one." I stood and started for the door. Pausing with my hand on the doorknob, I turned back to her. "You will let me know if I can do anything to help with your situation?" I waved a hand at the drink in front of her.

Adara grinned at me, mock clinking her glass in the air. "Oh, believe me, you'll be the first one I call."

I HADN'T LEARNED ANYTHING I could use from Adara. All I had were more questions. What could I do with the information that was given to me? I supposed I could do as Adara asked me, check in with my contacts to see what they knew.

But not Sid.

I think we both needed some time apart, and I was more than happy to give it to us.

Hopping back in my car, I headed toward the precinct. Sergeant Thompson might have some insight into the things happening around the city. Though he didn't know a demon's ass from a vampire's fang, he did have a nose for trouble.

I should have been more hesitant to go to the precinct. My last visit there hadn't exactly ended well. You can't really beat up a bunch of cops while on camera and come up smelling like daisies. However, in my defense, there had been a demon trying to push my buttons, and things could get a little out of control when demons were involved.

Stopping at the station, I parked and climbed out of my car. Before I made it two steps from it, a sharp throbbing pain shot through my head. I faltered on my feet, leaning against my car for support as I grabbed both sides of my head in agony. Then as soon as it came, it was gone.

What in the ever-loving fuck was that?

"Hey, you okay, miss?" A police officer I didn't recognize came up to me and placed a hand on my shoulder.

I blinked up at him for a long moment and then bobbed my head. "Yeah, thanks. I'm fine." I shrugged him off and started for the precinct again.

The officer called after me, "You sure you're not losing your mind, angel?"

I froze and then spun back around. "What did you say?"

The officer's brows furrowed as he frowned, his hands on his utility belt. "I didn't say anything. Are you sure you're alright, miss?"

My mouth pulled down into a deep frown, and I muttered to myself, "No, I'm not."

Pushing the weirdness aside for now, I walked through the glass doors to the precinct. The waiting area was filled to the brim with people. Either waiting to be taken back or waiting for someone to get out. It was overwhelming either way. The noise and push of aura made my head ache.

The door to the back opened, and Sergeant Thompson stepped out before I had a chance to go to the receptionist and ask for him. It was probably a good thing. She didn't exactly like me.

Thompsons large form, walked into the front his hands on the hips of tan slacks where his badge was pinned. He seemed more like someone who should be doing one of those sports the humans loved so much rather than commanding a bunch of officers. Though, I supposed the police force was as close to helping humanity as Thompson could get without being in the military. Thompson didn't seem like the time to like to be told what to do.

"Wiles." Thompson's eyes widened briefly before he smiled grimly at me. "I guess I don't need to call you to come in then. You know what's going on already, don't you?"

Taken back by his words, I shook my head. "Uh, no? I'm here for Adara." I glanced around the room before leaning toward him. "About a you-know-what problem."

Thompson jerked his head down once. "Good, then we have the same problem."

Confused by his words, I followed him into the back. The bullpen was just as busy at the front. Officers were working away at their desks or manhandling irate criminals. The lockup had more people in it than I'd ever seen before.

"What in the hell is going on here?" I asked, more to myself than to Thompson.

"That's what I'd like to know." Thompson ushered me into his office and shut the door. I didn't take a seat but stood by the window of his office, peering out into the bullpen. "We've had an enormous increase in violent attacks and other crimes in the last few days," Thompson explained, sitting down at his desk. "None of our analysts can explain it. There's no full moon. No new drug in the mix making everyone go crazy. It's just like hell itself decided it was time to play."

I twisted away from the window. "That's exactly what Adara and the Phoenix Guild are dealing with, except it's not just here. It's everywhere." I crossed my arms over my chest and peered back out the window. "Something is going on. Something big. I just wish I knew what."

Thompson sighed. "I guess that means we can't count on you to save the day for us?"

I arched a brow at him with a smirk. "You thought I'd just swoop in and make it all better? Isn't that *your* job?"

Shrugging his shoulder, Thompson shifted in his seat. "Well, this is more of a *'you'* thing than a human thing, don't you think?"

I threw my hands up in the air and walked away from the window to sit in the chair opposite of him. "Honestly, I don't know. It might end up being an everybody thing. We just don't know who's behind any of it. It might be retaliation."

"Retaliation? For what?" Thompson asked, lifting his coffee mug up to his lips.

"For going into hell and stealing back something that belonged to me," I told him with a flat look.

Thompson choked on his coffee, sputtering as he tried to get it back up. Once he was able to breathe again, he stared at me. "You went to hell? You can do that?"

I shrugged. "It's not easy, but yeah. I can. And they're probably pissed I fucked up their plans and are now trying to make my life even more complicated." I left out the part about Lucifer being in the mix. I didn't think Thompson could handle that big of a revelation today.

"So, what do we do?" Thompson asked, cleaning up the coffee he spilled.

I turned my head to the side, glancing back out the window. "Exactly what you're doing now. Your job. Leave the rest to me and Adara." I stood and made for the door.

Thompson clamored after me. "Hold on." His hand landed on my shoulder. "There must be something I can do to help."

My face pinched in irritation. "No, you can't. You're human. Deal with your human problems."

"Now, see here," Thompson countered, his brows furrowing together. "We've worked together on demon cases before. I don't see why we can't now?"

I shook my head and poked him in the chest. "See, that's exactly the problem. You don't see. You *can't* see. I'm the angel. *I'm* the one who has to figure all this shit out. You are just a useless human waiting around until it's time to die. So give your expiration date a break and stay out of it."

Thompson's jaw clenched, his face becoming red and puffy. "Maybe you should leave."

I nodded. "Maybe I should." I swung the door open and stalked out of the office, shoving past officers on my way out. No one stopped me or seemed to care. They were too busy with their own problems to worry about me.

It wasn't until I was outside the precinct that it sunk in what I'd just done. I had just alienated the only other help I had with the demons. Why had I done that? Thompson was right; he had been in the thick of things for a while now. There was no reason why he couldn't help now. In fact, that was the sole reason I'd come here. To get his help. So, why did I suddenly think that he shouldn't be in it?

Fuck. I dragged a hand through my hair and tugged on it. What the hell was wrong with me lately?

More and more, I was wondering if maybe Adara was right. Maybe Zee was influencing me, and I just wasn't noticing it. But how could that be possible? Until now, I would have said it wasn't. The fact that a demon was even housing up in an angel—an arch one at that—was unheard of, but being able to overpower my celestial aura to take over my body? Unbelievable.

Whether or not it was true, I needed to get this thing out of me. Sooner rather than later.

The only place I had left to go was where it all started in the first place. Back to Octavia's place. She would be able to help me get rid of Zee. Or figure out what the hell was going on. At least, I hoped.

DRIVING FURTHER INTO SOCAL was not what I had planned today. In fact, I hadn't had a plan at all today, and now that was coming back to bite me in the ass.

However, as I pulled up to Octavia's house, there was something peaceful about it. Something that made my insides calm. If there was anything funky going on with me then Octavia definitely had the remedy to stop it.

One could hope.

Octavia walked out of her house before I even got out of my car. Her tight, red curls were as vibrant as ever, and those all-seeing eyes scanned over me with a sympathetic smile.

"My, my, Mary, are we in a predicament." She tapped her cane before her as she shook her head.

I climbed up her front porch steps and smiled weakly at her. "Hey, Octavia, how are you?"

Octavia tut-tutted at me. "Now, you know you aren't here for that. So why don't we just bypass all the pleasantries and get down to it." She turned and wobbled back toward her door. "Come on, now. I don't have all day and neither do you." She gave me a pointed look before entering her house.

I sighed, straightening my back before following after her. The inside of Octavia's house was exactly as it had been before. Mismatched furniture and far too many items in the tiny place. There was already a tray with two cups of tea and cookies on a plate sitting on the coffee table waiting.

Sitting down in the armchair next to her, I asked, "So, you knew I was coming?"

"Of course I did." Octavia scoffed and handed me a teacup. "You know, for an angel, you're not very bright."

I scrunched my nose up and tried not to be too offended. "Sorry, I'm just . . ." I blew out a long breath. "Having a strange day."

Octavia bobbed her head. "Oh, I bet. Your aura is all kinds of out of shape."

I squinted at her, holding my teacup in both hands but not drinking it. "What do you mean?"

Octavia waved a hand at me. "I mean that mess of black spots. Your aura was whiter than newly fallen snow, and now it's got more spots than a Dalmatian. What have you been doing?"

I traced one hand down my form and tried to find the spots she was talking about. Unfortunately, I couldn't see my own aura without a mirror, not completely anyway. I hadn't even realized it was getting so messed up until she said something.

"Oh, dear. You don't even know, do you?" Octavia sat her cup of tea down and placed her hand on mine. "That's alright. We'll get you sorted out."

I relaxed a fraction from her words. "You can?"

She gave me a reassuring smile and squeezed my hand. "Well, I can certainly try. I'm not a miracle worker, but let's see what we can do. Now, finish up your tea, and then we'll get started."

We sat there in a comfortable silence while I finished my tea. That was one of the things I loved about Octavia, who I'd only known for a short time. She didn't feel the need to fill the emptiness as many humans did. Sometimes I wondered if she was really completely human at all.

Once I was finished, Octavia led me to another room in the house. This one seemed more in line with her line of work. Beads cloaked the doorway, making clinking sounds as we entered. The floor was covered with a colorful rug, and an altar sat to one side, lit candles, flowers, and little effigies lining the table.

I gave her a sideways look.

She shrugged. "What? You think you're the only supernatural beings in the world who need acknowledged?"

Choosing to ignore that argument, I moved further into the room, my arms wrapped around myself. "Okay, what do we do?"

"*We* don't do anything. *You* sit there." She pointed to the middle of the rug as she lit some kind of incense that burned my nose. I did as she asked and watched while she moved around the room. She did a few other things before kneeling before me, laying her cane down beside her. The bangles on her arms jingled with each movement. "Now, give me your hands."

Wary, I placed my hands in hers. I never did have much faith in this mumbo jumbo, psychic bit. They were a bit too unpredictable for my tastes.

For a moment, Octavia didn't do anything. Or at least, it didn't look like she did anything to me. Then my hands felt warm as if something were pushing into my skin. When it became unbearable, I screeched and jerked my hands away from her.

Rubbing my hands, I scowled. "What did you do that for?"

Octavia's expression darkened. "It's worse than I feared, Mary."

My annoyance melted away into worry. "What do you mean? What's wrong with me?"

Shaking her head, Octavia turned to the side where a cabinet sat. She opened the doors and dug through the inside for a moment. Pulling out a mason jar full of some kind of plant, she held it out to me.

"What's this?" I took the jar, perplexed by what I was supposed to do with it.

"This is a combination of things that I won't really get into now, but it will help keep the demon inside of you at bay."

My eyes jerked up from the jar. "The demon? What about it?"

Octavia sighed and looked at me sternly. "It seems that your demon is much cleverer than you thought. He has somehow bound himself to you, and I can't remove him. If you were at full strength, then perhaps you could destroy him or at least exorcise him yourself . . ." She trailed off and shrugged. "Be that as it may, make these into a tea and drink it every day. It will keep the demon in a catatonic state. It's a Band-Aid." She grabbed my wrist, locking eyes with me. "Not a fix. I suggest you find a way to get your full powers back—and fast—before the herbs no longer work on the demon."

"Will that happen soon?" I stared at the jar of herbs, worrying my lip between my teeth. "I mean, how long do I have?"

"It's hard to tell." Octavia rolled her shoulders. "It could be days or weeks. If the demon is a lower level one then it could be months, for all I know. But I wouldn't dawdle. The longer you wait to get back your full strength, the more likely the demon will take over your body completely, and none of us want that."

I inclined my head slightly. Octavia was right. The thought of a demon in a former archangel's body was not a pretty one. There were all kinds of chaos he could cause, not to mention what would happen if Asmodeus or worse, Lucifer, found out. They wouldn't need my consent to get what they wanted. I wouldn't have a choice or even know I was doing it before it was too late.

Thanking Octavia for the herbs, I made my way back to my car. This wasn't going to be an easy fix. Then again, when had anything in my time on Earth been easy? I did feel a bit more self-assured now that I had something to use against Zee. The only problem was how to get back to full power without my wings. I couldn't very well go back to hell. Not now, with everything going on, and I didn't know very many ways to restore my powers after the load I blew on Ramiel before. Usually, it just took time, and time was not something I had.

My phone rang in my pocket as I sat in my car. I placed the jar of herbs next to me in the passenger seat and pulled my phone out.

"Yes, Trisha?" I asked once I saw the caller ID.

"Hey, I need you back here ASAP. Where are you?" Trisha's voice sounded anxious and a bit alarmed.

My fingers tensed on the phone. "What's wrong? Did something happen?"

"No, nothing like that. I'm fine," Trisha hurried to explain. Then she muttered away from the phone. "Put that down. No, you can't play with it."

"Trisha?" I prodded with concern.

My assistant returned to the phone with an exasperated sigh. "Sorry, look. It's easier to explain when you get here. Just hurry."

"Well, I'm out in SoCal, so it will be a bit." I cranked my car as I said it, not wanting her to wait any longer than she had to.

"Fine. Fine. Just get here." She huffed into the phone before shouting at someone. "Hey, stay away from the windows. I mean—" The phone hung up before I could get the rest of what she was saying.

I stared at my jar of herbs longingly and shifted into gear. I guess my own problems would have to wait for a little bit. Let's just hope Zee saw it the same way.

SURPRISINGLY, I WASN'T PULLED over for speeding on my way back to the office. I had never driven so fast in my time on Earth. Though, knowing what I did, the police precinct was too busy dealing with real problems to bother with someone joyriding down the interstate.

I glared at the jar next to me in the passenger seat. This was all Zee's fault. He'd screwed me over with Sid and the police. I should be thankful he didn't fuck things up with Adara too. Though the lecher that he was probably kept him from bothering.

My car pulled up to the office with a thud, bumping the curb a bit more aggressively than I had planned. I threw open the driver's side door and bolted for the door leading upstairs to the office, the smell of Lou's following me as I went. My stomach growled, reminding me that I hadn't had anything to eat yet today. I promised it food as soon as I made sure that Trisha was alright.

Once up the stairs, I could hear the music playing so loud that it shook the very floor that I stood on. Laughter came from inside and then Trisha cried out, "No, don't do that!" Something crashed and I darted inside.

What I found was not what I was expecting.

I stared at the scene before me. Trisha's arms wrapped around the waist of a curvy, blonde woman, Trisha's face smushed into her cleavage. The woman danced and laughed as Trisha tried to get the large bottle of scotch out of her hand.

"Come on, Billie," Trisha urged the blonde in question. "Give it to me. You need to stay sober for this."

"Geez, Trish, lighten up a little." The blonde, Billie, giggled and patted Trisha on the head before trying to give her some of her drink. "Maybe if you drank with me then this would be more fun."

Trisha shoved the bottle away with a scowl. "It's not supposed to be fun. You're in real danger here."

I hadn't been noticed yet, not surprising since they had the music so loud, I marched over to the stereo and pulled the plug.

"Hey!" Billie swung around to where I stood and glared. "What's your problem?"

I dropped the cord and stalked across the room.

"Finally." Trisha sagged to the floor, releasing Billie as I approached.

Billie backed up from me, her face becoming concerned. I stopped in front of her so that our faces were inches apart. Taking up a human's personal bubble can be the most uncomfortable thing in the world—or so I'm told—I'd never had a problem with it.

I patted myself on the back for remembering that tidbit as Billie's face sank and she offered me the bottle.

"Drink?" she said, hopefulness in her voice.

I snatched the bottle from her hand and took a swig, letting the burn slide down my throat. "Now, sit." I pointed at the beat-up couch across the room that we used as a reception area. Billie crossed her arms over her glittery, silver dress and sauntered over to the couch. How she made walking in those four-inch heels look so easy, I'd never know.

Setting the bottle on top of Trisha's desk, I turned back to the two of them. "So, what's the problem? Why did you need me so quickly?"

Trisha stayed where she was sitting on the floor, her rainbow-colored, tulle skirt spread out around her. "Billie has a stalker."

"He's not really a stalker. More of an avid fa—."

"He tried to kidnap you," Trisha interrupted Billie, shooting a pointed glare at her. "Billie needs us to find the stalker."

"Fan," Billie jumped in but was quickly quieted by Trisha's death stare.

"As I was saying. We need to find Billie's stalker before her next concert." Trisha looked up to me with an annoyed sigh, but underneath it all was fear.

I gestured for Trisha to follow me into my office, but I kept the door open. I didn't trust that Billie to not do something else stupid like call her stalker a fan.

"What?" Trisha whispered, her eyes also flicking over to Billie every few seconds.

"How do you know Billie?"

Trisha sighed and pulled on one of her pigtails. "We went to school together before I got kicked out for hacking the teachers' emails and sharing all their personal information around the school." Her lips ticked up on the sides in memory. Shaking her head, she turned her attention back to Trisha. "We used to be really close. Then, you know, I got kicked out, and Billie won some national got-talent competition and skyrocketed to stardom."

I pursed my lips and glanced over to Billie. "She's a singer? I've never heard of her."

Trisha snorted. "That's not surprising. You don't listen to anything that I don't play, and I rarely hear you with the radio on in the car." She pointed toward Billie. "Billie has three platinum records and was named the new up-and-coming star to watch. She's come a long way from sneaking cigarettes in the girl's bathroom." There was that happy little smile again.

"So, a stalker? Why didn't she go to the police?"

"I can hear you!" Billie shouted from the couch. "I might be drunk and scared out of my mind, but I'm not deaf. And you don't know how to whisper."

Sighing, I walked back into the room and toward Billie. "So, why didn't you go to the police? I'm sure a woman of your . . . status." I threw a hand in her direction with a grimace. "Has security?"

Billie sneered. "I tried to tell the police, but they just blew me off. Apparently, they can't spare the man power to watch some silly little singer." She air quoted around the words.

Knowing what I knew, that wasn't surprising. All hell was breaking loose, literally. Billie's stalker was the least of their problems.

"And security details are so expensive these days. The guys I have are sufficient but . . ." She shrugged a shoulder and looked over her nails.

"Maybe if you spent some of that platinum-record money on a good security detail instead of your wardrobe then maybe you wouldn't be in this mess," Trisha pointed out with a snarl.

Billie huffed and dropped her hand. "You know, I came to you because I heard you had this tough-ass private detective as a boss. I thought you could help me out, but if all you're going to do is hate on me then . . ." She pushed up to her feet, not even wavering on those heels with the amount of alcohol in her system. Trisha cut her off at the front door before she could stalk out.

"Wait, wait." Trisha placed her hands on Billie's shoulders, keeping her from leaving.

"You're right. I'm sorry. I just don't want to see you get hurt."

Billie's shoulders slumped and her eyes watered. "Oh, Trishie," she cried, throwing her arms around Trisha's neck and pulling her into her chest once more. "I didn't realize you cared so much."

Trisha struggled against the hug for a moment before getting loose. "I just don't want to see my oldest friend hurt by some stupid stal—" When Billie opened her mouth to correct her, Trisha added, "Fan. Some misunderstood fan. Now, why don't you have a seat and tell Mary everything you told me?"

Nodding, her lower lip pushed out into a practiced pout, Billie made her way back to the couch. She sank down on it and leaned forward, actually looking serious about the situation.

I grabbed a nearby chair and sat across from her. "Why don't you tell me when this all started?"

"First off," Billie began, hiccupping slightly. "I want you to understand. Carl is not a bad guy. He's really sweet, you know.

Just not quite right in the head." She winced and rubbed her hands over her knees.

"Carl?" I arched a brow. "You know his name?"

"Oh, yeah. Carl Kauffman." She bobbed her head. "He's been a fan of mine since We've Got Talent happened." She smiled happily. "He was always there in the front row cheering me on, and then after every round, he'd send me big, beautiful bouquets of flowers."

"And have you and Carl ever met face to face before now?" I glanced back at Trisha to make sure she was getting this down. There wasn't a need. She was scribbling away as Billie spoke.

Billie shook her head. "Oh, no. Carl made sure to keep his distance. I was underage and all. It would look bad if he were too close to me, you know. But he'd send the sweetest letters and gifts. I always tried to wave at him whenever I performed."

"So, you encouraged his actions?" I prompted, trying my best to word the question. I didn't want her to think she deserved what had happened to her. No one asks to be kidnapped.

Shrugging, Billie played with her hands. "I was really new to fame and enjoyed the attention. I probably shouldn't have let it get this far, but he was always so sweet. I just didn't want to hurt his feelings."

"Have you ever met him one-on-one?"

"No way." Billie shook her head, her brows drawn together. "My parents would have a cow, and besides, I was way too busy with school and work to have much of a social life. I thank that for not being able to have any time to get sucked into the party scene of this life." She chuckled nervously. "You know, a lot of good talent goes down the drain because they can't handle the pressure and turn to drugs and alcohol."

I glanced at the bottle on the desk.

"Hey." Billie shoved at my knee. "I was just trying to blow off some steam. It's boring as fuck in here, and Trisha wouldn't let me touch any of your stuff."

I gave Trisha a grateful smile. "That's her job." I ran a hand through my hair and thought of what else I should know. This was the first stalker case of this magnitude I'd ever worked. "So, when did it all go bad?"

Billie shifted in her seat, not saying anything for a moment. "Well, I'd been under a lot of stress lately. It's hard to top so many platinums, you know? Everyone wanted to know when the next big thing was coming from me, and I might have vented a little bit to Carl."

My lips tipped down. "You contacted him? You have his address?"

Bobbing her head vigorously, Billie swiped a hand under her nose. "Sure. He always puts it in his letters, and I even have his phone number. He wanted me to know he was always there for me if I needed anything. So, when I was feeling really frustrated, I sent him a letter."

I didn't like where this was going. Though knowing the stalker's details—that was a lot more than I usually had on most of these cases I got. "What did you say to him?"

"That sometimes I just wanted to run away from it all. Be a normal girl for once. No paparazzies or having to hide when I go out." She rolled her head from side to side and then sank her head into her hands. "It was a moment of weakness, and now Carl thinks I need him to save me."

"Alright, I understand." I didn't, actually. How could she be stupid enough to tell something like this to someone so dedicated to her and obviously a bit crazy. Wanting attention was one thing but putting herself in danger this way was another thing completely. I wasn't sure how I was going to get her out of this one if she couldn't control her actions in the future.

"Where are you staying now?"

"Uh . . ." Trisha walked up behind me. "I thought maybe she could stay with you?"

I blinked at my assistant. "What, now?"

"I can't go back to my place," Billie interjected with a whine. "There's so many reporters there 'cause of the incident, and any place I rent or check in to will end up calling the media. Plus, Carl would never—" she glanced around the office with obvious disdain, "—never expect to find me here."

I pressed my lips together tightly before putting on my best customer service smile. "Will you give me a moment?" I stood and grabbed Trisha by the arm, dragging her to the other room. "What are you thinking? She can't stay here."

"Why not?" Trisha countered, tapping her foot. "You're armed. We have a couch." She grimaced and then added quickly, "I'll bring a blow-up mattress for her. And besides, she's right. No way in anyone's right mind would they look for her here."

"But what about the other problem?" I said through clenched teeth.

Trisha cocked her head to the side, confusion covering her face. "What problem?"

Oh right. I hadn't told her yet. I got bombarded by Billie the moment I walked in the door. I quickly explained to her what was going on in the area with all the demon activity as well as what Octavia had told me about the tea.

"So where's the stuff?" She looked me over, clearly searching for the jar.

I waved a hand toward the door. "It's in the car. I'll go get it later. I'm more worried about . . ." A snore, so loud a foghorn would be envious, filled the room. Twisting around to where Billie was passed out on the couch, I sighed. "Her." I rubbed the back of my neck and wondered how I got myself into this kind of stuff.

"You don't have to worry about her anymore. She's out cold." Trisha snorted and shook her head. "Not surprising. That girl can drink when she wants to. Now, how about that tea?"

I puffed out a long breath and handed her my keys. "It's in the front seat. I'll stay with . . . our charge." I stared at Billie with distaste as she snored again. "We're charging her extra for this, right?"

Trisha smirked as she got to the front door. "Oh yeah. Ten times the rate. Believe me, she can afford it."

I waved her off. "Great."

At least that would take care of having to worry about any other cases for a while. That was if I could get through the craziness going on in LA and get the demon out of my head before I died or worse.

THE SOUND OF CAR horns blaring shook me awake. I blinked at the morning light. Wait, where did the sun come from? Hadn't it just been night?

I grabbed my head where it throbbed and glanced around me. I wasn't in the office anymore. In fact, I had no idea where I was. It wasn't any part of LA that I recognized.

Just then, the car blared its horn again, and a man leaned out of his window to yell, "Get out of the street, you crazy bitch!"

Frowning at his words, I rubbed my temples again as I inched out of the street and onto the sidewalk. Once I was out of harm's way, I leaned against the nearest building. What had happened? Last thing I remember. What was it? Where was I? The office. Trisha had brought me a case. Billie. The singer. She was snoring so loud on my couch. Trisha went to get the tea and then . . . nothing. I remembered nothing.

Shit.

I bent over and put my hands on my knees, letting my head hang for a moment as I tried to get my bearings. That fucking demon. It had to be. I couldn't have ended up here all of a sudden for any other reason. He probably didn't want me to take the tea and suppress him. I scowled and swiped a hand under my nose. Something thick came off of my hand.

Frowning, I lifted my hands up. They were dirty and caked with a dark red-brown color. Dirt? I lifted my hand to my face and sniffed it. Not any dirt I'd ever smelled. I gave it a cautious lick and then just as quickly spit on the ground.

Blood. I had dried blood on my hands. Trying not to panic, I lifted my other hand and saw the same thing covering my skin and in the crevices of my nails. I touched my clothes, searching for where the blood might have come from. I didn't feel hurt. Had I gotten injured in some way? Maybe this was leftover from a fight? It wouldn't surprise me that the demon couldn't stay out of trouble. He was a demon, after all.

When I didn't find any injuries, something worse came to mind. What if the blood wasn't mine? There were a few places on my clothes where dark patches had dried. To someone on the outside, it might look like I'd been rolling in the dirt, but even with dark clothing on, I could feel it: the tacky feeling of blood caked to my skin from the dried places on my clothes.

There was too much blood for it to be from a fight. Not the kind of fight that ended with everyone going home in one piece.

My stomach churned and I spun around. I saw a convenience store and rushed in. The cashier behind the counter took one look at me and said, "Bathrooms are for paying customers only."

I dug into my back pocket and found some cash. Throwing it on the counter, I grabbed the bathroom key he had barely gotten out and darted for the bathroom.

Once in the bathroom, I flicked the lights on. My breath came in short, panicked breaths, and I was almost afraid to look at myself. Finally, I made myself stop and close my eyes. One long, deep breath in. One long breath out. Again. I did this until my heart didn't feel like it was about to jump out of my chest at any moment and then opened my eyes.

Approaching the sink mirror, I surveyed my face. No visible cuts or wounds. Not even a bruise. Though I could see where I'd wiped my hand over my face at some point, and blood had smeared there.

I turned the faucets on and pumped soap into my hands. I worked on cleaning the blood off my hands and out from under my fingernails first. I rubbed until my hands felt raw, but at least they were clean. Then I took a paper towel and wet it, cleaning the blood off my face. I couldn't do much about my clothes, not until I could get home and take a shower.

I stepped out of the bathroom and walked back into the convenience store where the clerk was looking at me not too happily.

"You can't just throw money at me. You have to buy something," The clerk snapped just as my stomach growled, reminding me that I had no idea how long I'd been out.

Searching around me, I grabbed a couple of bottles of water from the cooler and then the first bag of chips I saw and a protein bar. I threw them on the counter as my eye caught sight of the newspaper.

"Thursday? It's Thursday?" I gaped at the clerk in disbelief.

The clerk stared at me and then snipped, "Yeah. Maybe don't drink so much next time, lady."

Ignoring his sarcasm, I tried to wrap my head around the fact that I'd been out for three days. Two days of not knowing what I'd been doing. Two days of Trisha going crazy with worry. While I usually despised the little contraption, I would have killed for my phone right then.

When the clerk was done ringing me up, I asked, "Do you have a phone I can use?"

"There's a pay phone outside," he said as he shoved my change into my hand.

"Thanks," I grumbled. I chugged one bottle of water before I even reached the door and then ate the protein bar. I found the pay phone and set my other water bottle and chips on top of it. Thankfully, Trisha made me memorize the important phone numbers I would need after I lost my phone the first dozen times on the job. I put in the money and punched the number for the office. The phone rang three times before a peppy voice that was not Trisha answered.

"Mary Wiles Private Detective Services, what up?" There was a sound in the background like someone making a snarky comment which the speaker scoffed before adding on, "I mean, how can I help you?"

"Put Trisha on the phone."

"I'm sorry, Trisha is otherwise disengaged, but I would be more than happy to help you with whatever you need." The little giggle added to the end was all that I needed to realize who was speaking.

"Billie," I growled, my hand tightening on the phone handle. "It's Mary. Put. Trisha. On. The phone."

"OMG, Mary? Is that really you? We thought you were dead." Billie gasped and grew distraught before starting to ramble, "I woke up on your grungy couch where you were supposed to be protecting me, and then it turned out you weren't even there! I mean, what kind of PI are you?"

"Billie, give me the phone," Trisha snarled nearby, and there was a struggle for the phone that I assumed Trisha won because she spoke next. "Mary, where the hell have you been?"

I blew out a long breath and glanced around me. "That's what I would like to know."

Trisha went silent for a moment and then let out a long growl. "Alright, fuck. Just tell me where you are, and I'll come get you. We can figure the rest out when you're home and safe."

My brows rose in surprise. "What? No twenty questions?"

Trisha huffed a laugh. "Oh, I have questions. Tons of them. But let's just say it's been a stressful two days."

I nodded then remembered she couldn't see me. "I understand. And as far as where I am . . ." I searched for some kind of street sign and found nothing close. I grabbed the arm of a woman as she walked by. Her eyes widened at my appearance, and I quickly tried to reassure her. "I'm not going to hurt you. Can you tell me what street this is?"

The woman eyed me warily before bobbing her head and pointing. "You're on Airport Boulevard."

I released her. "Thanks." The woman hurried away as I returned to the phone. "I'm on Airport Boulevard."

Trisha hummed. "I know where that is. Can you be more specific?"

My gaze went to the convenience store I stood outside of. "I'm standing by a store called 24 Hour Grub."

"Gotcha. Hold tight. I'll be there shortly." Trisha hung up before I could say anything else.

Sighing, I hung the phone up and moved to stand against the wall. I watched people walk by as I waited, searching my mind for some kind of hint of what happened in the last two days.

The blood on me was old. At least enough to dry the way it had on my clothes and skin. Which meant at some point, I must have gotten into a fight or had been rampaging like demons tended to do. Strangely enough, I was hoping for the former. If Zee was fighting someone, then it meant there was a purpose to what he was doing and not just mindless violence. Strategic I could handle, crazy I couldn't.

TRISHA SHOWED UP ABOUT an hour later with Billie in the passenger seat. Trisha climbed out of the car and raced over to me, her arms open wide. I figured she was coming in for a hug and opened my arms to embrace her, only for Trisha to come up short once she saw my clothes.

"Uh . . . are you okay?" Her nose wrinkled at my appearance.

Dropping my arms, I brushed my hands over my clothes. "None of it is mine . . . unfortunately."

Trisha stared at me for a moment and then slowly said, "Right."

I scratched the back of my head, my scalp feeling dry and itchy. "Can we just get home? We can figure everything else out after I've showered . . . like ten times."

Jerking her head, Trisha grabbed my hand. "Right, come on." She led me to the back of the car and opened the passenger door. "Get in the back, Billie."

Billie gaped at her and then glanced back at me. "Ugh, fine. But I'm only doing it because I'm used to being back there anyway." She crawled out of the front seat and into the back. Once we were all seated, she grumbled, "It's weird being in front after all this time. This is more my place. Being driven around like the celebrity I am."

Trisha and I exchanged a look before Trisha quipped, "Yeah, yeah, and we'll get you back to being your big bad celebrity self in due time. For now, just sit back and enjoy the ride."

Billie snorted. "Not like I have much choice in the matter."

"Exactly," Trisha snapped, pulling the car onto the street.

I thought I was going to get a quiet ride back to the office. That was foolish. Not more than five minutes after we hit the road did Trisha start in on me.

"So . . . what do you remember?"

I opened my eyes from where I had been resting them and looked at her. "Really? Now?"

Trisha shrugged. "Hey, we have time to kill. Might as well be now."

I blew a hard breath out and rubbed a hand over my face. "I don't remember anything. So you might as well give up. The last thing I remember was you going to get the herbs from the car and Billie snoring on the couch."

"Hey!" Billie leaned over the back seat. "I don't snore!"

"Yes, you do," Trisha retorted and then turned back to me. "When I got back up to the office, the window to your bedroom was open, and you were gone. Billie was still sleeping, so she wasn't any help. I tried to call your phone. It rang a few times and then went to voice mail. Every time after that, it kept going straight to voice mail."

I hummed. "Zee must have gotten rid of it after you called. 'Cause I don't have it."

"Great," Trisha grunted. "Now we need to get you a new phone too."

"We also need to figure out what Zee was doing this whole time he was controlling my body." I peered out the window and murmured, "And how to stop him next time."

"We know how," Trisha answered me, shoving a jar at me. "You drink this crap like Octavia told you. Then we figure out a way to get that asshole out of you."

I took the jar in both hands and stared at it. Zee must have known that I was trying to suppress him, or he wouldn't have taken over just as Trisha went to get the herbs. Which meant that I couldn't be the one holding on to it. "Here." I handed the jar to Billie. "Don't let me anywhere near that."

Billie took the jar reluctantly as Trisha shoved her phone at me. "Here, call Adara. She's freaking the fuck out that you are missing. Not that she helped much when we called her for help," Trisha added on with bitterness.

Pursing my lips, I took the phone and scrolled to find Adara's number. I sighed and hit the button to call. The phone rang for what felt like forever before a snippy voice answered, "Phoenix Guild, Adara's phone."

Recognizing the no-nonsense voice, I held back my distaste. "Alec, it's Mary. Is Adara available?"

Alec clucked his tongue. "Adara is otherwise engaged, but I will be happy to let her know you have called. Have a good day." He hung up before I had the chance to say anything else.

I stared at the phone and wrinkled my nose.

"That was a short conversation," Trisha remarked with a frown. "What did she say?"

"I didn't get to talk to her. Alec answered the phone."

Trisha groaned. "Ew, that douchebag. If anyone needs to get laid, it's him. What'd he say? I reluctantly ask."

"Who's Alec?" Billie popped in from the back. I waved her off.

"Basically just blew me off. Said Adara wasn't available, and he'd pass on that I called." I flipped the phone over repeatedly in my hand. Something about the way Alec said it didn't sit well with me.

"Yeah, suuure," Trisha rolled her eyes and then shook her head. "I trust him to tell Adara as much as I trust box hair dye." She shot me a knowing look. "Which is not at all. So, now what? How are we going to find out what your alter ego did?"

My nose wrinkled. "Don't call him that. We aren't the same person. He's a parasite. It's different." I woke the phone up with my finger and brought up the address book. "The only other person that could help me find out what I did is Sergeant Thompson." My finger hesitated over the number. "But after what I said to him last time . . . I'm not sure he's going to want to help."

"Then we are basically screwed." Trisha sighed and then slammed her hand on the steering wheel.

I sat the phone down on my lap and bobbed my head. "I can't disagree."

"Hey, I thought you guys were the all-power duo?" Billie banged on the back of my seat. "If you can't even figure out what you did the last couple of days, how can I expect you to be able to protect me from Carl?"

I twisted around in my seat to look at her. "I meant to ask you, what do your people think you are doing right now?"

Billie flipped her blonde hair over her shoulder and leaned back in her seat. "That I'm at some all-inclusive health spa to get over the trauma of almost being kidnapped. But . . ." her eyes locked onto me, her gaze narrowing, "they won't believe it for very long. So, you need to start earning your retainer."

"Well . . . once I can figure out how to stop the demon inside of me from destroying everything then I'll be happy to work on your problem." I paused for a moment and then looked back at Trisha. "Wait a second . . . how does Billie even know about any of this?"

Trisha's lips twisted to one side. "Well, when you disappeared, it was kind of hard to keep it all a secret. Especially when someone . . ." Trisha glared at Billie through the rearview mirror, "wouldn't stop pestering me."

"And you're okay with all this?" I asked Billie with a cocked brow. "You're not freaking out like I expected."

Billie shrugged a thin shoulder. "I dated a Scientologist. So I've heard worse."

Huffing a laugh, I shook my head at her. "Not the same thing."

The rest of the ride was quiet, all of our minds focused on something else. Or mine and Trisha's were anyway. Billie kept prattling away about all the weirdos she'd dated before. We were both more than ready to get out of that car once we pulled up to the office.

"What's the plan now?" Trisha prodded as she climbed out of the car. "You get juiced up on that herbal tea and then what?"

I started to answer her and then my nose caught the scent of Lou's. "Actually, first . . . I need a little pick-me-up in the form of food."

Trisha groaned and hurried after me into Lou's shop. The scent of Chinese food grew stronger as the bell rang over the door we entered. Lou turned to greet us before grinning at the sight of me. "Mary! Where have you been? I have not seen you in a long time." His brow crinkled as he frowned. "You haven't been going somewhere else, have you?"

"Ew . . . you call this food?" Billie groaned, plugging her nose.

Lou gaped at her.

I waved her off. "Don't mind her. She's a food snob. Your food is still my number one. Promise." I put three fingers up before me. "Scout's honor."

Lou eyeballed my hand. "When were you ever a scout?"

I grinned and held my hands up in defense. "You got me. Never. But I would never lie about chow mein."

Laughing in agreement, Lou pointed at me and said, "Right. Right. One chow mein coming up. And for you?" He glanced at Trisha and then narrowed his eyes at Billie.

"I'll have my usual, Lou," Trisha grinned and bounced on her heels before shooting a look over her shoulder at Billie. "You better order something, or you're gonna go hungry tonight."

Billie took a step forward and then gagged. "Nope. I'm good. I'd rather starve."

Lou huffed and stalked away.

"If he spits in our food because of you," Trisha grabbed Billie by the upper arm, "you're dead."

"Believe me, that would be a blessing." She crossed her arms over her chest and scowled.

Trisha frowned and stared at Billie's hands. "Where's the jar?"

"Stop worrying so much. it's in the car," Billie snapped, jerking her hand toward the door.

Trisha shot me a look and growled through clenched teeth, "Billie," and darted out the door. I chased after Trisha and headed back to the car where the back door we had not locked was wide open and the jar of herbs Octavia had given me . . . gone.

8

TRISHA WHIRLED ON ME with a glare so hard that I swore she might shoot lasers through me like in the movies she made me watch. "This is your fault. You and your damn stomach. Why couldn't we just get the herbs in you and eat later?"

I raised my hands up in the air before placing my hands on my hips. "How was I supposed to know someone was going to steal the herbs? Not like I'm all-knowing."

"Yeah, you proved that," Trisha quipped, sarcasm dripping from her words. When Billie came up behind us, her gaze hardened even more. "You. Go up to the office and stay there. You will do what I say when I say it, and you won't complain, or I will throw you out on your ass, and Carl can have you."

Billie's eyes welled up with tears. "You don't mean that, Trish."

Trisha simply glowered.

I placed a hand on Trisha's arm. "Come on, don't say anything you don't mean. There's nothing we can do about not having the herbs, so why don't we just get our food, and we'll figure it out. Like we always do."

Trisha's gaze flicked from Billie to me, her lip ticking up on one side. "Isn't that my line?"

I patted her on the shoulder and then wrapped an arm around her. "You can't always be the optimistic one around here. I have to do my share every once in a while." I led her toward the office doors, but she stopped me before I could even open the door. "What?"

"Hold up, hold up. You . . ." she ducked under my arm and stepped back. "You aren't doing anything other than going upstairs and putting on those handcuffs you have in your desk drawer." She shot a look at Billie. "Billie can get the food." The diva opened her mouth to protest, but Trisha cut her off. "Count it as part of our expenses."

"What about Carl?" Billie whined, her eyes searching around as she shifted from foot to foot.

Trisha dug into her pocket and then tossed something at Billie. "Here, if he shows up. Spray him with that."

Billie glanced down at the item Trisha had thrown. "Pepper spray? If I wanted to protect myself with pepper spray, I would have done that at home, not come all the way out here."

"Hey, take it or leave it. Your choice." Trisha shrugged. "We have bigger problems."

I didn't get a chance to see what Billie chose since Trisha was ushering me up the stairs. "Geez, when did you get so pushy?"

"Since you disappeared on me for two days without a word," Trisha snapped back, giving me a good shove up the stairs. "Don't ever do that to me again."

I looked over my shoulder in the dim staircase. "You know I can't promise that, right?"

"What do you mean?"

"If we don't have the herbs to suppress Zee, then it might happen again. Not only that, but once I get my wings back, I'll . . ."

"Go back to heaven," Trisha finished for me with a frown. "I forgot about that. Hehe. You know, all this time I was worried about you ending up on the other side of town, and it never occurred to me that you wouldn't even be in this dimension anymore once you get your wings back."

"If . . . if I get them back," I corrected her with a weak smile.

"Like that's so much better." Trisha shoved past me.

I drew in a deep breath and then blew it out. Trying to keep my cool and not make it worse, I followed Trisha up to the office. When I arrived inside, Trisha stood in the middle of the doorway blocking my entrance.

"What are you doing?" I shifted to look around her only to see the wide shoulders of someone I hadn't seen or heard from in days. Well, I hadn't seen or heard from anyone in days, but that was beside the point. "Sid? What are you doing here?"

Trisha continued walking as if nothing had happened and went into my office, leaving the two of us alone. I could hear her digging around in my desk, slamming drawers and other things around. Guess I wasn't going to get away from that conversation any time soon.

Focusing back on Sid, who looked a bit worse for wear. He had shadows under his eyes, and his hands wrung together, tugging on the rosary around his hand and wrist. "I heard you were missing."

"I was." I stepped toward him, and he flinched. I stopped. "I'm back now."

"Are you okay?" He kept his gaze down, not looking me in the eyes as he spoke. "What happened?"

I wanted to reach out and touch him. To comfort him and let him know that I didn't mean it. That it wasn't me that did those awful things. Or at least not all me, but I didn't know how to put it into words. I didn't know how to make those shadows in his eyes go away. To make him not look at me with such . . . fear.

Using Trisha's favorite technique to defuse a situation, I tried to make light of it. "Oh, you know. Just the demon in me going for a joyride in my body."

Sid's eyes shot up, his brows drawn together. "That's not funny, Mary."

My face dropped. "I know. I'm sorry. This is kind of a bad time."

"Yeah," Trisha added on, joining us with the cuffs in hand. "So unless you want to be on babysitting duty, I suggest you get your ass out of here."

Sid glanced between Trisha and me. "Babysitting duty?"

I grimaced and explained the whole herb fiasco to Sid. "Yeah, so this is a precaution to make sure I don't go full Zee again."

Sid watched as Trisha cuffed me to the radiator in my room. "Are you sure that will hold you? I mean, you're an angel. You could easily break those cuffs in seconds."

Trisha shot him an annoyed look. "These are temporary. I'm going to get some rope and tie her to a chair or something." She straightened from where she was crouched and stalked toward Sid. "I have an idea. How about you keep an eye on Mary and make sure she doesn't go AWOL while I get the rope? Think you can handle that, Romeo?" She smacked him on the chest as she walked by. I didn't know where Trisha was going to get the rope and didn't ask.

I gave the cuffs a testing tug, frowning at their fragility. Leaning my head back against the wall, I sighed and closed my eyes.

"Should you go to sleep?"

My eyes shot open and over to Sid who had taken a seat at my desk. "What?"

"I mean if he's taking over your body. Wouldn't falling asleep be making you vulnerable?" Sid leaned forward, his legs spread apart and his hands cupped together between them.

I shrugged a shoulder. "I don't know. Zee seemed to be able to take me over pretty easily while I was awake. I don't think he really needs me unconscious to do what he wants."

"Gotcha," Sid responded before going silent.

"Besides," I continued, for some reason needing to fill the void, "he's probably regaining his strength after the last two days of mayhem. I doubt he'll resurface anytime soon."

"Oh."

The room fell quiet again, and this time I didn't try to fill it. After all the things I'd done and seen since my time on Earth, none of them were as painful as this very moment. Sitting here with Sid so close and yet a million miles away, it felt as if my wings were being ripped from my very being once again.

"Mary," Sid quietly said.

I lifted my head to meet his gaze. Those shadows were still there in his eyes but something else too. Hope.

"The other day . . . at the bar," Sid cleared his throat and looked away from me, his opposite hand clenching the rosary around his wrist. "Was that you or . . . ?"

"I don't know," I answered truthfully. "I've done a lot of things I wouldn't normally do in the last few days." I dropped my gaze to my hands. "I would like to blame it all on Zee, but I honestly don't know. Maybe it was me. Maybe it was Zee. Maybe it was a bit of both. All I know is that I felt terrible after it happened, and I'm sorry, Sid. I'm so very sorry." Tears burned my eyes, and I blinked them away since I couldn't wipe my eyes with my hands.

A hand touched my chin, lifting my head.

Sid kneeled before me. "That's all the answer I need." He leaned down, and his lips brushcd mine.

"Jesus," Trisha complained, walking into the room, her arms full of ropes. "Get a room."

Sid and I smiled at each other before glancing around the room.

Trisha rolled her eyes, dropping the ropes on the ground. "Right." She clucked her tongue. "I walked into that one. Can you stop making out long enough to help me tie up your girlfriend?"

"We weren't making out," I explained and then snapped the cuffs apart.

"Told you," Sid said, arching a brow before taking my hand. "And yes, I'd love to tie you up."

"Ewww." Trisha wrinkled her nose. "It's like listening to my parents talk about sex. TMI."

"You started it," Sid reminded her. He held out my desk chair for me. "My lady."

I smiled and sat down. Sid and Trisha brought the ropes over as Billie walked in the door, her hands full of bags. "Don't ever ask me to do that again." She stomped across the room and plopped the bags on the desk. "Lou made me try several different dishes to prove to me that his food was perfect before he would give me your food. I can feel it trying to fight its way back up as we speak." She shuddered and grabbed at her stomach before staring at us. "What?"

Trisha just chuckled and began wrapping the ropes around me.

The ropes tightened around my form. Something soaked into my clothes, causing a chill to run through me. "Why is it wet?"

"Holy water," Trisha explained, handing the next rope to Sid to wrap. "Make sure it's tight. And this way, even if you are strong enough to break the ropes, the holy water will slow Zee down . . . hopefully."

I nodded. "Good idea. But you know this is only a temporary solution right? I can't stay tied up forever."

"I know," Trisha huffed. "That's why I'm going back to Octavia to get more herbs while Billie watches over you."

"Me?" Billie cried out, practically stomping her foot. "Why do I have to do it? She's supposed to be taking care of me, not the other way around."

"Don't worry. I'll stay too," Sid chimed in, causing Billie to blink as if she'd just seen Sid for the first time.

"And who is this delicious piece of manwich?" Billie purred, sashaying toward Sid, a flirty look on her face. She held out a hand to him. "I'm Billie. As in Billie, the singer."

Sid stared at her outstretched hand. "Uh. Sorry. I don't listen to much modern-day music."

Billie pouted her lips. "Oh. Well." Her eyes brightened. "We have lots of time—I'm assuming—since Trisha has to go get some more of those voodoo herbs, right? I'll sing some for you."

Sid shot me a look that screamed "help me."

My lips twitched at the ends. I said nothing.

Trisha smirked and backed away after tying the last knot. "You guys have fun with that. I'll be back as soon as I can."

I stretched my neck to follow her with my eyes. "Hurry back."

"No, no," Billie called out, grinning at Sid. "Take your time. We have everything we need right here."

"AND THERE'S NO GOING back nooooow," Billie ended her song with a big flourish of her arms and a wide smile.

Sid clapped politely.

I opened my mouth to tell her that was enough singing for now. Except what came out of it wasn't even close. "Oh, my fucking god, just exorcise me now and save me from having to listen to another minute of your putrid singing."

Zee?

"Hey!" Billie curled her fingers into little fists and stomped her foot. "I know my music isn't for everyone, but I'm a paying customer. The least you could do is pretend to like it."

A snort came out of my mouth. "Is that what your stalker Carl tells you?"

"Mary?" Sid leaned over me, his eyes locking with mine.

I tried to tell him that it wasn't me, but I couldn't get the words out. I shifted my head from one side to the other. Relief filled me. At least I had control over my body, if not my mouth.

My lips curled up in a way I'd never felt before. The sight must have been disturbing to see because Sid stepped back from me.

"Sorry," Zee's singsonged with my voice. "Mary can't come to the phone right now, but if you leave a message, she'll get back to you . . . never." My head fell back as Zee laughed and laughed.

I tried to jerk my hand to get Sid's attention. The ropes were too tight, and Sid was too distracted by what my mouth was saying to pay any mind to my hands.

"Zee," Sid sighed and squared before me. "I was wondering when you were going to show yourself."

Billie inched closer to me with a curious fear in her eyes. "That's the demon?"

"In the flesh, sweetheart." Zee cackled and then added on, "Well, sort of." Jerking my head back to Sid, Zee moaned, "I was taking a nice little nap in Muriel's subconscious until this one," he jerked my head toward Billie, "would not stop that awful racket. It's enough to make me want to rip my own ears off. Or well . . ." my lips ticked up wickedly. ". . . Muriel's. You know, I've never been in control of an angel's body before. It's quite . . . fun." Zee licked my lips and skimmed his gaze over Sid salaciously. "Tell me, Sid, was it good for you?"

Sid straightened to his full height, his hand coming up into a fist. "So, it *was* you pulling the shots."

Zee shrugged my shoulders. "What can I say? You're too much of a goody-goody. So worried about hurting someone, you can't embrace your full self. I was just trying to help you out."

Slamming his hands on either arm of my chair, Sid brought his face inches from mine. "The only thing you did was piss me off and make Mary feel bad."

"Ugh," Zee scoffed, rolling my head back from Sid. "Don't give me that crap. I'm inside of her. I know how she feels better than you do. And let me tell you a little secret, Sidney," Zee enunciated his name, leaning closer to him as he lowered my voice. "She liked it."

Sid shoved away as Zee cackled. I'd never heard myself cackle; it was quite disturbing to hear.

"Should we call Trisha?" Billie asked, rubbing her arms up and down with her hands.

Shaking his head, Sid moved to the other side of the desk. "No, the demon might be making Mary talk, but he doesn't have the strength to do anything else. Especially not with those ropes being drenched in holy water."

Zee shifted in my seat, testing the ropes out. "You know, it does itch a little. Nothing like when I was riding that human before though. Must be those nifty angelic powers."

He lifted my hands, I assumed to pull at the ropes. I shoved them down. Zee frowned or I frowned. Whatever. Anyway, he tried again, and I pushed them down once more.

"Mary," Sid jumped in hopefully, "are you still in there?"

Zee shot a glare at Sid. "She's being stubborn. If she'd just relax, then this would all be over with."

I pursed my lips in annoyance.

"That!" Billie pointed at me. "That's Mary's facial expression."

"Mary," Sid tried again, coming around the desk and grabbing my hands. "Come on, baby. Fight it. Shove that demon back where he belongs."

Zee snorted. "You should know. You have a lot of experience with that, daddy's boy."

Sid ignored Zee's jab and spoke at me directly, squeezing my hands. "Come on, Mary. I know you can do this. Just focus on me. Grab my hands tight. I got you."

I tried to do as Sid asked, focusing all my attention on him and his hands. The warm, rough feel of his fingers on mine. The way they knew how to make me feel like more than just an angel stuck on Earth. Like someone important.

Zee fought me. He pushed at my consciousness. I blocked him out, shoving him down as far as he could go.

"That's it," Sid encouraged, giving my fingers a squeeze. "You can do it."

When Zee was pushed all the way down, it was as if a weight had lifted from my chest, and I could finally breathe. I gulped up lungfuls of air and blinked rapidly.

"Sid?" I grabbed his hands more firmly. Happy that I could move my own mouth again, I took a big breath and threw my head back and let out an aggravated yell.

"Hurry, it's still the demon!" Billie shouted, moving as far away from me as possible.

Sid laughed. "No, it's not." He moved his hands from mine and cupped my face. "It's Mary again."

"What's all the yelling for?" Trisha asked with furrowed brows. She walked across the room, her hands carrying the one thing we needed more than anything. The herbs.

"Thank fuck," Billie cried out, rushing to Trisha's side. "That demon came out again."

"Are you alright?" Trisha asked Billie, and then before Billie could answer, turned to Sid and me. "Did anyone get hurt?"

I shook my head. "No, he didn't get that much control. But . . ." I wiggled in the ropes. "I don't think the holy water in these ropes is going to do any good if he does get full control."

"I agree." Sid bobbed his head. "He didn't even act like they bothered him."

"Well, it doesn't matter anyway," Trisha said, bringing the jar over to the desk. "Because I have our solution right here."

"You mean our Band-Aid," I corrected her and jerked my head toward the jar. "Octavia told me that won't keep the demon down forever. Eventually, he'll get used to it, and it won't even stop him a little bit. We need to get him out of me."

"Yeah . . . about that," Trisha drew out with a hesitant look. "I don't think we should get rid of him . . . not yet anyway," When I started to object, she added on quickly, "We want to know what the bigwigs are up to, don't we? Who's calling the shots and making a mess down here or up here?" She paused and tugged a piece of her hair. "I'm always confused by that."

"It's more of an overlapping system," I reminded her. "There is no up or down. We are all on the same level, just different planes of existence."

Trisha moved over to the coffeepot and poured out the coffee before starting it to make some hot water. "So, the whole falling from heaven isn't technically a fall?"

I shrugged a shoulder as best I could tied up. "Not really in the physical sense. You can fall from one dimension to the other, so in that sense, yes, you are falling, but in the literal sense, no."

Bobbing her head, Trisha brought a coffee mug over to the desk and unscrewed the lid. She scooped out some of the broken-down herbs and put them into the cup. Then she walked back over to the coffeepot and poured what little water had been in it into my cup. My nose crinkled up at the smell of the herbs mixing with the water and just a hint of coffee. Hard to get rid of it completely when you're using a pot specially made for it.

"Are we sure we want to do this now?" I asked as Trisha brought me the cup. "If we still need him to figure out what's going on, maybe we should wait?"

"Is that you talking or the demon?" Sid questioned, placing a hand on my shoulder.

I shot him a look. "Me." Then to Trisha, I said, "I'm all for keeping him suppressed, but we don't know how long that will last, and what if one of his cronies comes to check on him?"

"How do you know he has any cronies?" Billie asked, chewing on one of her nails.

"Someone had to have stolen the first jar," Trisha reminded her with a scowl. "It didn't just get up and walk away."

Billie frowned. "Right."

"Here," Trisha shoved the cup across the desk. "Drink up."

I stared at the cup and then back to Trisha, arching a brow.

"Oh." She laughed before picking the cup up and handing it to Sid. "Sorry, forgot."

Sid blew on the cup to cool it down before placing it near my mouth. I grimaced. It smelled even worse this close up. Huffing out a breath, I took a tentative sip and regretted it instantly.

"That bad, huh?" Trisha retorted, her lips twisting to one side.

"Worse," I coughed out before forcing myself to drink some more of it. I downed the whole thing, swallowing as much as I could handle before it tried to come back up again. Sid sat the cup down on the desk and stayed by my side, waiting.

It took a moment for my stomach to settle, and I was confident enough to nod at Sid. "I'm okay. I think you can untie me now."

Sid glanced over at Trisha, who only shrugged before beginning to work on the ties. Once I was free of my confines, I stood and stretched. When I felt the dried blood pull at my skin, I made a face.

"What? What is it?" Trisha leaned forward, ready for anything I threw at her.

I scratched my side and scrunched up my nose. "I think I should probably shower before anything else goes wrong."

Everyone looked at me for a moment before laughing nervously.

"Yeah, definitely." Sid offered me his hand. "Let me help you with that."

I shook my head and ignored his hand. "No thanks. You seem to be a trigger for you-know-who, so I think I'll deal with this one alone."

Sid's face drooped in disappointment before he sighed and tucked his hands into the pockets of his jeans. "Alright, well, if I'm no longer needed here. I'm going to go check on the bar. Maybe I can get some information out of the regulars about what Zee's been up to."

I bobbed my head and stripped my shirt over my head. Sid stopped by me on his way out the door to plant a kiss on my forehead.

"Be careful," he murmured to me.

I peered up at him with a soft smile. "I will. I'll call you if anything comes up."

"Speaking of which," Trisha interjected pulling something out of her pocket, "I got you a new phone." She held it out to me with a stern look. "Think you can go a day without losing this one?"

"Not likely," I told her truthfully. "But stranger things have happened."

10

I SCRUBBED MYSELF SO hard that I was sure that I'd taken a few layers of skin with me. It was worth it to get the remains of whatever Zee had been doing off of me. I just had to keep him at bay long enough to get him out of me.

You won't get rid of me that easily, love.

I groaned in annoyance as his voice bounced around my consciousness. "Go away," I said out loud and stepped out of the shower. I grabbed a towel and began drying off.

Sorry, no can do. I'm on a deadline, and you're messing up my schedule.

I snorted as I wrapped my hair up in the towel. "Why don't you tell me your plan, and then maybe I can help?"

I wasn't born yesterday. I'm not going to tell you, an archangel, what my lord's plan is. You'd just try to stop me.

I shrugged a shoulder. "True. Can't argue with you there."

"Mary," Trisha knocked on the bathroom door. "Who are you talking to in there?"

I turned and opened the door. "Just trying to convince Zee to tell me the master plan."

Trisha took one look over my nude form and sighed, "Well? Did it work?"

"Sadly, no." I rubbed my face with the side of my towel, dropping it when I heard a gasp. Billie stared at me. Or rather, at my nether region. "What?"

Billie gaped for a moment longer and then met my gaze. "You have genitals."

I frowned and exchanged a look with Trisha. "Uh, yeah. What did you expect?"

She lifted her hands in a shrug. "Nothing. Flat like a Barbie doll. You know . . . like in the movies."

Trisha blew out a hard breath. To me, she said, "Mary, put some clothes on. Billie, let's go in the other room and check in with your people."

Billie reluctantly went with Trisha, but not before telling me, "You know, pubes are so last year."

I glanced down at the junction between my legs and frowned. I shrugged and walked into my room. I threw my ruined clothes into the trash can and grabbed some new ones. Once dressed, I took a seat at my desk and opened my Chinese.

Sid had tried his best to feed me while I was tied up, but after a few fumbling attempts, I just told him I'd wait until Trisha got back. Now I was starving. I didn't even bother heating up the cold chow mein before scarfing it down like a wild animal.

Ew. Slow down. I might be a demon, but even I have manners.

I snorted. "Then why don't you tell me what you were doing with my body the last few days?"

Not gonna happen. Zee's voice was a singsong in my head.

"Fine," I quipped through a mouth full of food. "I guess I have to figure it out the hard way."

Guess so.

Scowling at the demon, I finished my meal and then turned to my computer. Flicking the mouse to wake it up, I clicked over to the LAPD database Trisha had hacked into at one time for me.

I searched for any deaths or strange happenings over the last few days in the area where I had woken up.

Gunshots fired.

No. While I had no problem using a weapon, they didn't seem to be Zee's style. He seemed more the type to want to get his hands dirty. Or rather, mine.

Robbery.

No.

Six bodies found on North Central and Rosecrans brutally murdered and ripped apart. No witnesses. No suspects. The police think it's in connection to the other murders that have been going on around LA.

That sounded promising.

I clicked on the folder holding the pictures from the scene. Just like one of the cases Thompson had showed me; these body parts were being staged in a way that spelled out something.

"Care to shed some light on what I'm looking at?" I asked the demon inside of me.

Nope.

"You know it's a message for me. It'd be easier to tell me." I tried to be persuasive as I flicked through more pictures.

Where's the fun in that?

"Oh, so it *is* a message." I smirked at Zee's sound of disappointment. "Just tell me instead of killing people. You know pen and paper work just as well."

Zee chuckled darkly. *The bodies are the message.*

"To what?"

He wants it back and he wants you.

"Who does?" I asked, even though a pit formed in my stomach. I didn't want to voice my opinions. I'd rather Zee tell me himself.

Oh, you know. Zee chuckled once more before whispering so that the next word echoed through my mind. *Lucifer.*

Trisha popped her head into the office. "Find anything?"

"Nothing new." I clicked the X on the page and closed it. Making Trisha worry about what I'd done wouldn't help right now. Zee had confirmed my suspicions, and that only made me want to keep Trisha out of it even more. In fact, if the devil was involved, they all needed to stay as far away as possible. "What about you? How'd it go with Billie's people?"

Trisha sighed. "They need her to come in for a costume check, and since we haven't caught her stalker yet, we have to go with her."

I grimaced. "Great. That sounds . . . fun."

"Right?" Trisha quipped leaning against the inside of my door. "Why don't you get some sleep? I'll keep an eye on Billie tonight. Then we can head to over the set tomorrow."

"Are you sure?" I stood and walked over to her. "You must be running on fumes yourself." I reached out to touch her tired face.

She dodged my hand and grinned. "Hey, I can sleep when I'm dead. Besides, I'm not the one who has to take down a stalker and stop a bunch of demons from killing us all. I can afford to lose some sleep. You can't." She gave me a little push. "Now, go to bed."

For once, I did as she asked. I didn't feel tired but knew that I'd been running on demon fuel the last two days. So, while my mind may not be tired, my body probably was. It proved it once my head hit the pillow, and I was out.

When I dreamed, it wasn't the same nightmare I always had. The sound of laughter, the searing pain in my back, and the never-ending darkness. This time, the screams weren't coming from me, and I was the one holding the knife.

"Please, no. I have children!" The woman before me cried, tears streaming down her face.

My mouth curved into a smile as I swung the knife. "Good. They're next."

The woman screamed so loudly that I jerked awake.

Sitting straight up in bed, I rubbed my eyes with the palm of my hands. The room was dark, and the sound of the TV came from the other room.

Just a dream. It was just a dream. I let out a slow breath and lay back down. I lay there and closed my eyes, not really wanting to go back to sleep but not having much choice in the matter.

I didn't lay there long before there was a scratching sound coming from the window. Frowning, I sat up once more and grabbed my gun from my holster by the bed. I crept over to the window and slowly grabbed the bottom of it before flinging it open, my gun pointed at the intruder.

"Don't shoot! It's me!"

I leaned in closer to get a better look and found Adara on my fire escape, her hands high and a bag slung over her shoulders.

Lowering my gun, I stepped back from the window, allowing her to enter. "Why didn't you use the front door?"

Adara brushed her pants off and dropped her bag on the floor. "Those bastards at the guild would be watching the front door for me. So, I came in through the side."

I pursed my lips and crossed my arms, my gun still in my hand. "And why are you hiding from your own people?"

Adara blew out a hard breath. "That fucktard Alec started a coup and decided that he would be better fit to run the guild than me. I'm supposed to be on house arrest until they can decide what to do with me." Adara hopped up on my desk, swinging her legs. "And so, here I am."

"You know this is the first place they're going to look for you," I reminded her as I holstered my gun and turned on the nightstand light.

"Nope. I told them I wasn't speaking to you anymore 'cause of the whole demon-inside-of-you deal." She smirked and flicked her hair over her shoulder. "Pretty smart, huh?"

"Well, I still have a demon inside of me, and it's been trying to send me a message from a big bad. So, I'm not exactly the best person to be around right now."

Adara picked up my left-over container of Chinese and sniffed it. Shrugging, she dug into it, as voracious as I must have been earlier. "Better than being there with that bunch of hypocrites. Besides, you weren't the first place I went."

"Oh yeah?" I sat on the edge of the bed and pulled on my shoes. Guess I wasn't getting any more sleep tonight.

"Yep, I went to several of my safe houses. Made myself a real paper trail for them to follow. It should take them a few days to figure it out. And hopefully by then, I will have a plan."

I arched a brow. "One can hope."

"What about you?" she asked, picking at the food now before setting it down. "Where were you?"

I grimaced. "That's what I'd like to know. But unfortunately, my current source of information is being a tight-lipped dick."

Zee laughed inside my head.

"Ah, so I was right." Adara bobbed her head.

"As you often are."

"So, what's the plan?"

I leaned on my knees with my elbows and stared at her. "What makes you think I even have an inkling of a plan?"

Adara scoffed. "'Cause you're you. I know there's something going on in that cosmic brain of yours. So, fess up."

I shook my head. "Sadly, at the moment all we can do is wait for one of Zee's cronies to show up."

"So you can capture it and make it tell you everything," Adara said while picking her teeth with one of her nails.

"Yeah. But until then, we have real clients we have to deal with." I gestured to the closed office door. "One of Trisha's friends from school has a stalker."

"That's no fun." Adara hummed. "I always wanted to be famous enough to have a stalker, but no one likes me quite that much."

I sighed. "Apparently, she's some big singer. Billie something or other. Though if you ask me, her singing could use some work."

Adara gaped at me.

"What?"

"Billie? The best-singer-on-this-side-of-the-planet Billie? Is here right now? In the other room?"

"Uh . . . yes?" I cocked a brow as I watched Adara almost hyperventilate. I'd never seen the badass vampire hunter so excited before.

Adara jumped off the desk and ran across the room, throwing the office door open and screeching like one of those fangirls. "Billie!!!"

11

"ALRIGHT, YOU GO OVER there. And you get Billie's clothes brought out. We need to see how everything fits before the concert." Bea, as she had introduced herself to us a few moments ago, commanded the room the way a captain commanded his ship. No one questioned her, and everyone hurried to do her bidding. Even Billie seemed hesitant to complain.

Bea turned to Billie and then frowned at us. "Do you have to be here?"

Placing a hand on the edge of my holster, I eyeballed her sternly. "Billie's safety has been compromised. We can't chance her coming out in the open like this alone."

Lifting her hands up with a scowl, Bea shook her head and walked away.

"You know," Billie twisted in her seat to look at me, "you really don't have to be here. There's tons of people around. There's no way Carl will make a move while I'm here."

I scanned the room, taking in all the entrances and exits. How nobody was questioning whether anyone else was there. "This is just the place that a stalker could easily slip in and out of. I wouldn't be doing my job if I left you defenseless."

Billie snorted, turning back in her seat so the hair and makeup artists could work on her. "Like you haven't already done that."

"Yes, well, that won't happen again," I reassured her, though the look Billie shot me was anything but reassured.

Trisha tapped me on the shoulder. "Why don't we let Adara watch over Billie, and we'll go see if we can hunt down Carl? This might be the perfect moment to snoop around his place."

"Yes, totally. I'd love to hang out with Billie." Adara beamed and gave a clap of her hands. I gave her a look that made her quickly return to her bodyguard stance. "Uh," she cleared her throat and jerked her head once in a nod. "I mean, of course, I will make sure that no harm comes to our client. Leave it to me."

I pursed my lips and frowned. "I'm not sure that's such a good idea."

"Oh, it'll be fine," Billie said, waving away my concerns. "Carl has never shown up for a fitting. He does have some manners."

I arched a brow.

"Ugh, okay, so maybe kidnapping me on the way to my car was not showing manners, but still, I've never seen him around here. You should be fine."

"Should be is what I'm worried about," I muttered and then faced Adara. "If you see anything, you call me, okay? Don't leave Billie alone. No matter what."

Adara snapped to attention and mock saluted me. "Aye, aye, captain."

Sighing at how I got myself into these kinds of situations, I followed Trisha out of the building and back to our car. Trisha pulled up her phone and typed in the address for Carl's place.

"Wow, that's a nice area," Trisha commented with raised brows.

I pulled onto the street and said, "It goes to show you that even rich people can be crazy, and in my experience, so far they're the only ones really allowed to be."

It didn't take too long to get to Carl's. I half expected Adara to call before we even got there, but as we pulled up into his driveway, I was sadly disappointed.

Trisha gaped up at the house before us with wide eyes. "Whoa, I guess he could give Billie the life she's used to, at least."

I climbed out of the car without responding. Normally, I'd park down the street and wait until the cover of darkness, but since Carl had given Billie his address, it showed he expected someone to show up eventually.

"Do we just knock?" Trisha asked, placing her hands above her eyes to shield herself from the sunlight.

"Think anyone would answer?" I walked up the stone pathway to the two-story home that looked like it should have been in one of those home and garden magazines and not the home of a crazy stalker.

Stopping at the front door, I cupped my hands around my eyes and peered into the window lining the door. "Lights are out."

"Maybe no one's home?" Trisha asked hopefully.

"Does he have any family?" I questioned, reaching into my pocket for my lock pick set.

Trisha shrugged. "Not that we know of. He's an IT guy as far as Billie or anyone else knows. The cops don't have any wife or kids on file, so it could be just him at the house."

I lifted my head briefly to look up at the house. "Pretty big house for one person."

"Maybe he was waiting for Billie," Trisha offered up, leaning on the doorframe beside me.

The door clicked and swung open. An alarm beeped right inside the door, waiting to be disarmed. Turning to Trisha, I asked, "Any ideas what his code could be?"

Trisha sighed and stepped up to the keypad before typing in a few numbers. The alarm instantly stopped beeping. I stared at her until she said, "Billie's birthday. It wasn't that hard to guess."

I bobbed my head. "Gotcha. Don't use birthdays."

We walked into the house, closing the door behind us quietly. Not turning on any lights, we had to rely on the sunlight pouring into the large windows to light the way. Which wasn't particularly hard since there were so many windows.

"The guy does not care if his neighbors see into his house," Trisha muttered, glancing out the nearby window. "And he is just too neat for my liking. Definitely a psycho. "

I snorted a laugh. "You can't tell that by how clean someone's house is. He might be a neat freak."

Trisha shot a look over her shoulder. "Like I said, psycho."

"There's nothing in the living room. I'm going to check the other rooms; you keep a look out." Trisha nodded in response, and I made my way up the stairs and into the first bedroom. This one was as picturesque as the rest of the house. The bed was made with fresh linen. The room smelled of lavender and as I pulled open the closet, I realized it was unlived in. Frowning at the empty closet, I went to the dresser and opened the top drawer. Empty as well.

Could it be a guest room? Trying not to read too much into it yet, I moved on from the first room and into the bathroom. This one had a fcw items. A toothbrush. Some toothpaste and mouthwash. One towel. And a comb.

Not touching anything, I went back into the hallway where Trisha met me at the top of the stairs.

"Anything?"

I shook my head. "Not yet. You're right though, this house is way too clean."

"I told you so." Trisha poked me on the shoulder and followed me into the next room. This one was slightly different than the others. The blankets were rumpled, and there were shoes discarded on the floor. But the one big thing that stood out to us was the wall covered in pictures and clippings from newspapers and the internet—all about Billie.

"Wow, guess that means we have the right house," Trisha murmured, moving closer to the wall. "Look, he kept all Billie's letters she sent him." She pointed at a section covered in single sheets of paper with loopy handwriting on it. "At least she wasn't lying about writing him back. You know, very few celebrities actually do that."

"I'll remember that for the future," I said dryly. "Now look for something that might tell us where he is or what his plan might be. We need to find him before he tries to take Billie again."

We hurried through the room, opening drawers here and there. Trisha dug under his bed while I tackled his closet. This one wasn't empty. It was stuffed full of plaid shirts in every color they could possibly come in.

"Holy plaid!" Trisha exclaimed, coming up behind me. "What is this guy? A lumberjack?"

I pushed his clothes aside and searched behind them. Most people weren't as smart as they thought they were with their hiding spots. Those places you see on television shows and in the movies? Yeah, the bad guys saw those same ones too. So, hiding something in the back of the closet was one of the first places I was going to look.

"Look at this." I withdrew a folder with a date three days from now. Inside were several papers and a printed-out blueprint of a building.

Trisha leaned over my shoulder and grabbed the blueprint. "That's the place Billie's concert is going to be at."

"And here's the security schedule." I showed her the paper underneath. "Well, at least we know when he plans to grab her next. Hopefully, we can stop him this time."

The humming of the garage door alerted us.

"Crap!" Trisha shoved the blueprint back at me and scrambled for the bedroom door. "It must be Carl. What do we do?"

I closed the folder and placed it back where I got it and then closed the closet doors. "We're not going to panic," I told her firmly, my hand going to my gun. "This is perfect."

"Perfect?" Trisha gaped at me, her eyes wide with panic. "How is this perfect? We're gonna get caught."

"If we grab him now, we don't have to worry about catching him before he tries to kidnap Billie again." I held my hand up to her as I crept into the hallway. I unclipped the holster of my gun and withdrew the weapon, holding it in my hand at my side as I moved down the hallway.

Whoever was coming in wasn't making much noise. A set of keys clanked on the counter. I inched down the stairs, waving Trisha off as she tried to follow too close behind me. When I got to the bottom, I pressed my back up against the wall and waited for Carl to come closer. Footsteps moved in on me, and I lifted my gun, holding it with both hands as I rounded the corner.

"Hands up!" I called out. I was met with a loud screech not by Carl—but a woman.

"Please don't hurt me! I'm just the housekeeper."

12

"JESUS FUCK, MARY!" TRISHA came up behind me and grabbed my arm, pushing my gun down. "She's the housekeeper."

Eyeballing the woman warily, I lowered my gun but didn't put it away. Why would the house cleaner come in through the garage door?

"If you're looking for the valuables, I don't know where they are." The woman shook her head, her hands still up and her eyes flicking down to my gun every few seconds. "I just clean the house. Which honestly doesn't need much work."

"We're not robbers," Trisha told her and then shot me a warning look. "We're private detectives."

"Why do you come through the garage?" I pointed out with a narrowed gaze. "Don't housekeepers usually come in through the front?"

The woman's eyes shifted from Trisha to me before saying, "The client requested it. They change the number every day." She reached for her bag, and I lifted the gun. "I'm just getting my phone to show you." She pulled her phone out of her bag and showed me the screen. "The client texts me a new code every time I come. I don't even know their name."

I frowned. "And the shrine to the singer, Billie, upstairs isn't strange to you?"

Her eyes widened and then she shifted in place. "I'm not allowed in one of the rooms. I'm supposed to clean downstairs, the first bedroom, and the bathroom. Nothing else."

Trisha sighed. "So, you can't help us."

"Sorry." the woman shrugged. "I wish I could be of more help. Is he dangerous?"

I holstered my gun and met her gaze. "Only if you're Billie." Turning to Trisha, I tapped her shoulder. "Come on, let's head back. We're not going to learn anything else here. We'll just have to wait and see."

"Ugh," Trisha groaned out, crossing her arms and stomping her feet all the way to the car. "I hate waiting. There's too much left to chance, and I'm worried for Billie."

"Me too." I stopped at the car, not getting in. "Do you think Billie would cancel the concert until we could get a hold of Carl?"

Trisha snorted. "Do pigs fly?"

I frowned. "Uh . . . no?"

Trisha and I climbed into the car. Placing her hands on the keys, she didn't turn them until she asked me, "Do they fly in heaven?"

"What?" I blinked at her. "No. No. We don't even have pigs."

"Oh." She cranked the car and then turned to me again. "Then what do you do about bacon?"

I squinted at her. "What? We don't. No bacon. No pigs."

Pulling out of the driveway, Trisha let out a long sigh. "Well, that's disappointing."

"Can we just get back to the fitting? I don't like leaving Adara alone with Billie for too long. She might get too distracted by the singer to do her job right."

Trisha's eyes shifted from the road briefly. "You don't think Adara would be professional about this?"

I arched a brow. "You know we're talking about Adara, right?"

Trisha shook her head. "Just because her bed partners are questionable—" she grimaced. "—it doesn't mean that she doesn't take her jobs seriously."

My phone rang. Pulling it out, I glanced at the screen. "Speak of the devil." Trisha snorted. "Adara, how's it going? Billie still alive?"

"Oh my god, Mary." Adara gasped into the phone, her barely contained excitement coming through the phone. "This is so cool. Why don't you let me help you on jobs more often?"

"You're a vampire hunter, Adara," I reminded her with a side-eye look at Trisha.

"And you still didn't answer me about Billie. Is she alive? Any sign of Carl?"

"What? Oh, pfft. No. Billie is fine. She's doing her thang, and that's a big no on the Carl-o. How about you two?"

I sighed. "Nothing on our side besides what we already suspected. Carl's going to try and snatch her at the concert." I leaned against the door and tried to see if I could get Adara's support. "What we should do is—"

"Don't you dare say cancel the concert," Adara interrupted me with a growl. "Do you have any idea how important this concert is to not only Billie but her fans? We *need* this concert."

I clamped my mouth shut and clenched my jaw. What was with these humans and their celebrities? They're just people. You didn't see me panting after every commanding officer in heaven. If I did that, we'd never get anything done.

"Fine. Then how do you think we should go about making sure that Carl doesn't grab Billie at the concert?"

"I think—"

Trisha leaned over and called out, "That doesn't involve you being on stage."

Growling into the phone, Adara grunted, "Fine. Kill all my fun."

"Don't do anything. We'll be back shortly." I hung up and told Trisha, "You better drive faster. I'm not sure Adara can manage this."

Trisha grimaced. "You got it."

The ride back to the fitting took forever. I hadn't been this antsy to get somewhere since the day they announced the new squadrons a millennia ago.

"Would you stop that?" Trisha snapped, unbuckling her seat belt. "You've been tapping your foot the whole way. It's driving me nuts."

"Sorry," I dropped my leg. "I hate waiting for something to happen too. Waiting for Carl to make a move. Waiting for Zee to give away his plan or one of his cronies to show up. Everything lately has been about waiting."

"Waiting to go back to heaven . . ."

I glanced over at Trisha who avoided my gaze. "Yeah," I murmured. "That too."

"Come on, Billie is probably ready to let Carl take her after spending time with

Adara." Trisha climbed out of the car. I watched her leave, not moving to follow her just yet. I didn't know how to make Trisha feel better. She knew from the beginning that my whole goal was to get back to heaven. I'd never planned on staying. I also hadn't planned on falling in love with Sid or being such close friends with Trisha or Adara.

Plus, there's no Chinese food in heaven.

Taking a deep breath, I got out of the car and walked toward the building. Once I stepped inside, I knew something was wrong. There weren't as many people in the room as before. In fact, the lights had dimmed, and the room was basically deserted except for three figures. As I approached, my feet slowed, and my hand went to my gun.

Billie, Adara, and Trisha I recognized. The back of the man standing before them, I didn't. Though, from the way that Trisha and Adara had stiffened, it wasn't someone we wanted there.

"I don't know why you guys are freaking out," Billie laughed, standing up and moving over to the man. "This is my good friend,

Dash. The famous actor? Don't tell me you don't know him."

"Get away from him, Billie," Trisha told her friend, taking a step toward her. "That's not who you think."

Adara pointed her gun at the blonde-haired man as I came closer. "What are you doing here, you bottom-feeder?"

"Now, now, no need to be feisty. I'm not here for you anyway." The smooth voice of Asmodeus, a voice I'd never forget the rest of my life, then called out, "Muriel, please join us."

My gun pointed at his head, I moved around him, giving the demon lord a large berth until we were face to face. "What an unpleasant surprise."

"You don't look happy to see me." Asmodeus smirked in the handsome actor's body he was still riding.

"Why would I be happy to see you?" I kept my gun trained on him and darted my eyes over to Billie, who was far too close to the demon lord for comfort. "Billie, get away from him."

Billie scoffed. "You guys are crazy. This is Dash. We've been dating for like forever." She shook her head and grabbed Asmodeus's hand, throwing an arm around his shoulders. Even without heels Billie was a head taller than him. She dragged her hand through his hair and grinned at him. "Don't you read any gossip magazines?"

"Yes." Asmodeus clasped her hand with his and smiled maliciously. "Billie and I have been together for over a year now."

"How'd you find us?" I prodded, trying my best not to let him affect me.

Asmodeus stroked the side of Billie's face lovingly. "Why Billie of course. She posted a lovely picture of her and her new best friend," he shot a look at Adara. "They looked so delectable that I had just had to come and see this fitting for myself."

Billie giggled and snuggled into Asmodeus's side.

I couldn't help the disgust that covered my face. The idea that Billie was having intercourse with a demon lord just made every part of me feel . . . icky. Not to forget it was just wrong.

Thankfully, I wasn't the only one feeling the ick factor. Trisha pulled out her phone and clicked on it a few times before showing it to Billie. "Your boyfriend is possessed by a demon lord. This one to be exact. Notice the horn." She pointed at her phone with vigor.

Billie leaned in slightly to stare at the picture, her brows wrinkling as she looked at it. "Is that a horn for its . . ."

"Penis," Trisha ended for her. "Yes, it is. That's what you've been banging this last year, 'cause that's about how long we've been trying to stop Asmodeus's skeevy ass from taking over the world and bringing literal hell to Earth."

Billie looked to Asmodeus and then back to us. I could see the wheels turning in her head as she processed what we had told her. Did she believe the people she had just met and one who she had known since school? Or the hot actor guy who she'd been boinking for the last year? I could see the problem. If I were her, I'd have a hard time choosing as well.

The singer opened her mouth to say something, but a sickening crack, followed by the light fading from her eyes and Trisha's screaming, interrupted her. Billie's head twisted to an unnatural angle as she fell to the ground in a crumpled heap.

Asmodeus adjusted the cuffs of his suit and laced his fingers before him. "Well, then, where were we?"

"Why?" Trisha gasped, kneeling on the ground a few feet from Billie, afraid to get too close. "Why would you kill her?"

Shrugging with utter disinterest, Asmodeus said, "She was annoying. I was done with her."

I glanced over at Adara, who hadn't said anything. Her eyes were on Billie's prone form, her mouth gaping open. Was she in shock?

"Well, you got what you wanted. Why are you still here?" I snarled at the demon, my finger itching to pull the trigger. It wouldn't kill him, but it would hurt like a bitch, and that was enough for me.

Asmodeus stepped over Billie's body, tucking his hands into his pockets. "You think I am here for her? Oh no. This is all about you. And what you have been fighting against this whole time."

"Don't come any closer." I put the barrel of the gun between us. "I will shoot you."

"Oh, please do." Asmodeus grinned. "Alert the security guards of my dear girlfriend's demise. Oops." He playfully pressed his fingers to his lips and corrected himself. "Ex-girlfriend."

"You're a sick bastard, you know that?" I quipped, practically shaking to pull the trigger.

"Mary," Adara warned, placing a hand on my shoulder. "Remember we need to know what they know, and we were waiting for one of Zee's cronies, weren't we? What do you call him?"

Asmodeus threw his head back and laughed. "You think, you think . . . I'm one of Zee's lackies?" He wiped the tears of laughter from his eyes. "That's too precious." Clearing his throat and adjusting the flaps of his suit jacket, Asmodeus declared, "I'm afraid you are incorrect in your assumptions. Zee, as you call him, works for me." His teeth gleamed as he gave us a nasty smile.

I shrugged a shoulder. "Not surprising. You always did have a way of worming yourself into places you shouldn't be. Why wouldn't this be the same? I bet there is no stalker, huh? Carl one of yours too?"

Waving a hand between us, Asmodeus shook his head. "Oh no. Sadly, I can't take credit for that one. Our girl really did have some crazy fans." He glanced back at her almost forlornly. But I wasn't fooled.

"Don't call her that," Trisha snapped, glaring up at Asmodeus from the ground. "She wasn't your girl. You used her for your sick games with Mary and then threw her away when she was of no use to you. So, in no way was she ever *your* girl."

The demon lord chuckled. "I see you haven't lost your bite, little one." He moved over to her and knelt down to murmur, his fingers playing with the strands of her hair, "I can't wait to play with you next."

"Not before I see you in hell," I spat out.

Asmodeus glanced away from Trisha and back to me. "My dear, that is precisely the point. See, I'm only here because our mutual acquaintance has run out of time. Zee," he made a face at that name as if it tasted bad in his mouth, "was supposed to get you to hell to deliver the blade, and he failed to do that."

"What does that matter?" I scowled at him. "You can't use it. I could hand it over to you right now, and it would be nothing but a piece of metal to you and Lucifer."

"Lucifer?" Adara's head jerked to me. "The devil's in on this now?"

"Sorry, I was trying to keep you out of it," I bit out before turning back to Asmodeus. "You want Michael's blade? Fine. You can have it. So, call off your dog."

Clucking his tongue, Asmodeus languidly walked around the area, playing his fingers along everything he came across. Brushes, dresses, wigs that Billie was supposed to wear for her concert. It didn't feel right to see him touching her things like that. "You see, Muriel, you're right. I can't do jack shit with the blade without an active arch angel to use it."

I snorted, ready to tell him I told you so.

"Don't get too excited just yet," Asmodeus waved his finger at me. "Because that's where you come in. You come to hell with me—with the blade, of course—and open the gate to heaven for us."

"Why would I ever do that?"

Asmodeus smirked. "I'm so glad you asked." He stopped by Billie's form and nudged it slightly with his foot. "Because if you don't, Billie won't be the last body you bury. Not to forget all those other bodies piling up." He tut-tutted, looking to Adara. "You and the police sure have your hands full. Wouldn't it be nice to know who was doing it?" A malicious grin crept up his face as his eyes slid over to me. "It would be so easy to slip a surveillance video of a certain private eye butchering all those people, and I am, if anything, a law-abiding citizen. It would be only right of me to do my civic duty in catching a serial killer."

We gaped at the demon lord as he practically cackled with glee.

"Mary didn't do any of those things," Adara snapped, her hand lifting the gun back up. "I know she didn't do them."

"Ah, but do you think your guild will agree with you? They don't particularly like

Muriel . . ." Asmodeus's eyes slid from me to Adara. ". . . or you right now, do they?"

I didn't bother asking him how he knew any of that. The asshole apparently had spies everywhere. He had us and he knew it.

"Now, now, I am generous after all." Asmodeus backed up, his hands held up as if to stave off some attack. "I will give you time to decide. After all, we have to honor our fallen friend." His gaze darted down to Billie and then back to us. "You have until after the funeral to decide. Then the gloves, as you say, come off."

My finger played on the trigger of my gun as the smarmy jerk turned his back on us and walked away. Trisha stopped me this time. I turned to her with a frown.

"He's not worth it. Besides," she lowered her gaze to Billie. "We're going to have enough problems as it is explaining how we are the only ones around when Billie died."

She was right.

Fuck.

13

"WHAT DO WE DO now?" Trisha stared down at Billie's still form, her arms wrapped around herself as if she couldn't bear to look away. "Call the cops?"

I holstered my gun and ran a hand over my face. "I guess, but I'm not sure exactly what we're going to tell them. We can't really start with oh, a demon lord killed her and then ran off, and none of us shot him first."

"I mean . . . it's the truth," Trisha tried to smile hopefully and failed. "Maybe Thompson could help?"

Adara pulled her phone out with a sigh. "I'll call the lawyer."

"Good idea," I told her, taking my own phone out. Thompson may not help us, but it would be better if we told them what happened versus them finding out.

"I'm surprised you had the guts to call me," Thompson growled into my ear. "Have you called to apologize?"

"Oh, yeah." I chewed on my lower lip. "I forgot about that. Actually . . ."

"You forgot how you insulted not only me but every single member of this police force? Why would I want to help you?" I'd never heard Thompson so angry at me. I probably should do something to make it up to him, but . . .

"Look." I sighed and held a hand up. Might as well go for it. "I've got a dead body."

Thompson harrumphed. "And how is that my problem? Call 911—that's what they're there for."

I winced. I deserved that. "It's one of my clients."

"Again," Thompson barked into the phone, "I don't know how that's my problem."

"Mary." Trisha grabbed my arm tightly to get my attention. "Hurry up! The security guard is coming."

I turned to where she was looking and groaned. Damn it. "Okay, fuck. Thompson, I didn't mean what I said. I'm having some issues with a demon who's not making my life easy right now. I need you to help me out here 'cause if I get locked up, there's going to be a lot more dead bodies to deal with. Got me?"

Thompson was quiet.

Just then, the security guard noticed us and Billie's body on the ground. "Hey, you! Don't move! I have a gun."

"So do we," I called back at him, only for Thompson to groan into the phone. I could practically see him put his face in his hand.

"Mary, don't say anything else. Where are you?"

I told him the address to the building.

"I'll be there shortly."

Hanging up the phone, I tucked it into my pocket before turning to the security guard, who apparently had called some friends because they were coming in behind him. "I'm holstering my gun and reaching for my badge." I nodded to Adara. "Put your gun away."

Adara did as I asked and also dug into her back pocket and pulled out a plastic card just as the security guards approached us.

"My name is Mary Wiles. I'm a private detective. I was working for . . ." I gestured to Billie's body, "the deceased."

Trisha stifled a cry. Finally coming out of her shocked state.

I placed a hand on her arm, pulling her closer to me. Partly for comfort and partly to protect her from the guards. "This is my assistant, Trisha, also a friend of the deceased, and this . . ." I pointed to Adara, who held her badge up.

"Adara Smithson, private detective. I was here assisting Mary with her case."

I tried not to make a face at the obviously fake name Adara had given.

The security guard took both of our badges and looked them over while his friend held their little taser guns up at us. "Alright, but no one is going anywhere until the cops come."

"I already called them," I told him and then jerked my head toward the body. "Can we step away from the ... body? It's distressing my assistant; they were friends."

The security guard looked down at Billie's body and snapped his fingers. "Damn it. Not Billie." He looked over at his friends. "I just got backstage passes to her concert for my girls."

His friends didn't seem as upset by the pop singer's passing.

"Let's come over here," the first security guard instructed with a sniff. I didn't know if it was for the singer or for the loss of money. We followed him over to the back part of the room where there weren't any exits. I guess he didn't believe us as much as I thought.

We waited in an awkward silence for the police to get there. When we finally heard the sirens in the distance, we all visibly relaxed. Finally, the cavalry was here.

Except when they came barreling through the door, they had their guns drawn, and it wasn't Thompson who was leading the troops but Riley.

"Shit. Fuck," I cursed under my breath.

"What is it?" Adara asked as they surrounded us.

Trisha saw who was coming, too, and muttered, "Trouble."

"Mary Wiles," Riley crooned. "I never thought I'd see the day that I would catch you red-handed. I always knew you were a killer, and now I can prove it." He gestured a hand at Billie's form. "Like them young, I see."

"Fuck you," I spat out with a snarl. "You know I didn't do it. I called it in."

"Smart thinking." Riley bobbed his head, walking toward us with his hands on his hips. "Call in the murder so you can get the heat off of you. It's almost like you think you have some kind of magic power over the police force here, but I'm here to tell you, that's not how this works." He jerked a hand toward us, telling the police by him, "Cuff them."

"Where's Thompson?" I asked as they slowly approached me. Seems some of them still remembered what I did at the precinct the last time they tried to arrest me. "I called him, not you."

"You don't worry about that. Just worry about yourself." Riley grinned, entirely too happy with himself. "And here I thought this week was going to suck."

"What do we do, Mary?" Trisha asked as the police began to cuff her.

"Stay calm. We've done nothing wrong," I instructed as I held my hands up to show the officers I wasn't a threat. "Adara called her lawyer. We'll get out of this in no time."

Riley laughed. "Yeah, just keep telling yourselves that. But we've got you for more than just this one."

I gave him a flat look. "I don't know what you're talking about." Did Asmodeus go ahead with this threat even though he had given us until after the funeral? He was a demon, after all. It wouldn't be a surprise to me if he had lied.

No. He would be here to gloat. This was something else. Just had to figure out what.

The cops took us out of the room with Riley laughing the whole time, patting himself on the back for doing such good work. I could tell he was pushing Trisha's buttons since she was the most affected by the death of Billie.

"Don't let him get to you," I reminded her as we got into the squad car. "He's just being a dick to make himself feel better."

"It's not that," Trisha whispered back. "My mom is going to kill me when she finds out we got arrested. Forget being killed, this is waaaay worse to her. I'll never get to work with you again." She gasped in horror. "She's going to make me get a real job!"

I scrunched my nose. "What you do *is* a real job."

Trisha arched a brow. "Really? We basically just take pictures of people doing it for money. I'm talking corporate. I'd have to wear slacks. Me! In slacks!"

Shaking my head, I settled into the car. Thankfully, Riley didn't ride with us. I didn't think I could take any more of his self-praise. The guy needed to just go jerk one off and get it over with.

"Man, I can't believe you guys offed Billie." The officer in the passenger seat said, glancing into the back. "She was one of the only female singers I could stand nowadays."

Trisha jerked forward in her seat so her face was pressed against the mesh that separated us. "We didn't do it."

"Sure you didn't," the officer chuckled. "We know your friend's record. It was only a matter of time."

I twisted my arms to the side so I could touch Trisha. "Hey, don't say anything else. They're just trying to get a rise out of you. Just wait until we get to the precinct. It'll be okay."

"Yeah, just keep telling yourself that," the officer chuckled again.

The ride to the police station was even worse than standing over Billie's dead body. The tension was so high that it was rippling off my aura. I didn't even need to use my powers to see how agitated everyone was. Well, not the cops, anyway. They were practically glowing with excitement. I guess they were some of the ones who didn't particularly like me at the precinct. Oh well. Can't please everyone.

"Here we go. Hope you know who your first phone call is," the officer said as he pulled us out of the car, "'Cause you're gonna need it."

It only got worse from there.

When we walked into the precinct, the room was full of demons. They cackled and clapped as they saw me pass. I glowered at them, which only made them laugh harder. A few of them catcalled Adara. I shot her a look.

"What?" She flicked her head so her hair fell over her shoulder. "What can I say? I'm hot to every species."

Trisha and I exchanged a look before rolling our eyes.

The moment we walked into the back room, the entire room of police broke into applause. I kept my eyes straight forward and resisted the urge to break the cuffs and beat the hell out of every single one of them. Not too long ago, the majority of them were working side by side with me to take down a group of demons. Now, they were cheering for my arrest.

"Well, well." Riley met up with us in the middle of the room. "I guess you aren't as popular as you used to be, eh, Wiles?"

I didn't bother to answer him. I didn't want to add fuel to the fire.

Adara, on the other hand, had no such issue. "Yuk it up now, chuckles. 'Cause we're going to be out of here before you can give yourself that ill-deserved circle jerk."

Riley grinned and crossed his arms. "We'll see about that. Separate them. I don't want them trying to collaborate their stories."

I nodded at Trisha, telling her to be strong. Adara and I didn't need to exchange anything. We knew what we were doing. We could handle ourselves. Besides, I'd been tortured before. This couldn't be any worse.

14

CUFFED TO THE METAL table before me, I tried to keep as calm as possible. This wasn't anything new. I'd been here before. This wasn't the first or last time Riley would try to get me on something. This time shouldn't be any different.

I hoped Trisha was doing alright. Adara, I wasn't too worried about. I highly doubted this was her first time either. To be frank, it wasn't really Trisha's either. Though I supposed being up on murder charges was far different than hacking the government systems. One was far more significant than the other, but which one depended on who you asked.

I sat there for what felt like an hour, though I knew it couldn't have been more than ten minutes. They wanted me to stew, and not having a clock in the room made me feel the pressure. It was a basic interrogation technique. One I'd used many times on the demons I hunted. Though they cared far less about waiting than the humans did. We lived forever, after all.

"So . . ." The door slammed open with a bang, and Riley appeared with a file in his hands. "I knew I'd get you back in this room eventually. It was only a matter of time."

I cocked my head to the side, watching him as he moved to the other side of the table. "You don't have any other cases to work on?"

Riley grinned maliciously, placing his hands on the back of the chair before me. "Not any that are as big as you, Wiles." He slapped the file on the table between us and pointed at it. "So, tell me, do you get off on killing people or just the torturing and maiming?"

I frowned. "I don't know what you're talking about."

Snarling, Riley flipped the folder open and pulled out the pictures inside. I viewed at least a dozen pictures exactly like the ones that Thompson had shown me before, as well as new ones that were very similar to that of Adara's.

The pictures weren't new. What was new was the fact that I now knew that Zee had done this with my body. I swallowed down the bile that threatened to come up and blinked at Riley. "What of it? Thompson already told me about the killings."

Slamming his hands down on the table so that it shook beneath my hands, Riley glowered at me across the table. "Don't pretend that this isn't your handiwork. We already have your name written all over it."

My lips twisted to the side. I knew I probably should keep my mouth shut and wait for the lawyer to come, but he really had my interests peaked. "What do you mean?"

Scoffing, Riley pulled a few pictures out and lined them up. "Like you don't know. Your name is written all over the victims."

I really looked at the photos now, squinting as I tried to piece together what he was talking about. It took my mind a moment to catch up to what he was pointing out. There, on several of the bodies that had only been slashed, were letters. At first glance, you wouldn't realize it until you placed them side by side like he had. The first two spelled out the letter M, the next two an A, and then on and on until it spelled out the word Mary.

Shrugging, I pushed the images away from me. "So? That could be any number of Marys. I'm not the only one with the name, you know."

Riley's teeth gnashed together. "Ah, but not everyone goes by your other name." He pulled out a few of the images where the bodies had been ripped apart and lined up. "This one spelled . . . 'Muriel.'" I forced my face not to react at the name. Riley paced before me as he spoke. "See, I've been asking around about you, Mary, or is it Muriel?

Which one do you prefer?" He didn't wait for me to answer. "You seem to know an awful lot of criminals, and they all seem to hate your guts so much—they practically begged to tell me what your real name was."

I stared at him, neither denying it nor admitting it. He was trying to catch me up, and I wouldn't let him. I had no memory of these murders. Not in my conscious mind, anyway. My dreams . . . that was another story.

Looks like someone's in trouble.

Great. Look who decided to show up.

Want some help?

Not from you, I don't. Why don't you just go back to where you belong?

Oh, no, no, Muriel. That's not how this works, and you know it. Besides, your little herbal remedy is wearing off, and soon you will have no choice but to let me out.

I grimaced.

"What? Too close to the truth for you?" Riley asked, practically beaming with self-satisfaction. "Just admit it. I have you by the short hairs. You aren't walking away from this one."

Not giving him the satisfaction, I leaned across the table, gesturing for him to come close. Riley, in his hubris, did just as I expected. I smiled, opening my mouth and stating, "I want my lawyer."

Shoving away from the table with a snarl, Riley shouted, "You will get a lawyer when I'm damn well ready." He rounded the table and got right up in my face. "I will get you for these murders and a whole lot more, I'm sure. Don't think Thompson can save you this time."

"I wouldn't be so sure about that," Thompson answered from the doorway. He held the door open and gestured for Riley to exit. "Come on, Riley, you know the rules. This lady wants a lawyer. You can't deny her that."

Riley looked at Thompson and then back to me. He seemed sorely tempted to say screw the rules and continue, then all of a sudden, he pushed away from the table and stalked to the doorway. Pausing before Thompson, he got inches away from the large man's face, something few dared to do. "This isn't over. She's guilty, and I'm going to prove it."

Thompson nodded. "Then do your job and prove it. Don't antagonize the perp."

Riley shot me one more glare before storming out. Thompson closed the door after him, walking toward me. He sat across from me with a sigh. "I'm sorry about him. When they found out you had a dead body on your hands, Riley jumped all over it with this new lead. I have a feeling he's been holding on to it for the perfect time."

I snorted. "Not surprised. What about Trisha and Adara? They're not part of this. Why not let them go?"

Thompson bobbed his head and sighed. "Unfortunately, since you're being held under suspicion of the murders, they're going to want to keep them to question them—not only about Billie's murder but the others."

I winced. "Trisha hadn't heard about the murders. Adara's group already knew. Some of those pictures I'd already seen before. And I'll tell you now . . ." I leaned forward and lowered my voice. "There are a lot more than that."

Thompson blew out a breath and dragged a hand over his head. "I'm going to pretend you didn't tell me that. This is about to go out of my hands, Mary. Do you need anything that I can actually help with?"

I opened my mouth to tell him to get my lawyer when Zee took over.

"You can get that ugly mug out of my face. Bring back the hottie. Riley, was it?" My lips curled up to the side. "Now that is one tasty piece of pig meat."

This time, instead of getting angry, Thompson eyeballed me. "Mary? Is that you?"

My mouth spread wide, and Zee singsonged, "Guess again."

"Shit." Thompson shoved his chair from the table and backed away. "Come on, Mary. Tell me what you need me to do."

"I told you," Zee continued with glee. "Get out of here and get the hottie back. I feel frisky. You have no idea how pent up this body is." Zee moved my hands up to my chest as much as he could while cuffed to the table.

I fought against Zee's control, trying to get a word out to tell Thompson what I needed, but Zee was a lot harder to control this time than before.

Since I couldn't control my mouth, I forced my hands to grab the notepad Riley had left and gestured for a pen from Thompson. At first, he didn't seem to realize what I wanted, distracted by Zee's ongoing crooning about what he wanted to do to Riley. When he finally got the picture, he pulled his pen from his pocket and shoved it into my hands.

"I'll make sure that Riley knows how much you admire him," Thompson mentioned, keeping Zee's attention as I scribbled on the paper.

"Admire him?" Zee scoffed with my voice. "I'd hardly call it admiration. All you flesh bags are lucky my kind doesn't devour every last one of you. Nothing more than monkeys in clothing." He shook my head, making my hands jerk slightly as I wrote. "What's this?" Zee tried to take over my hands. I shoved the pad of paper toward Thompson before he could get it. "Hey, what does that say?"

Thompson took the paper and glanced over it. "Really? That's what you need?" He arched a brow, cleverly not saying out loud what I'd written. If he did what I asked, then I could at least get rid of one thing that was going to make things worse.

I gave him a thumbs-up and then jerked my hand toward the door, indicating for him to go do it now. Zee was getting stronger, and I wasn't sure how much longer I could control him. The last thing we needed was for a demon to be rampaging around the precinct in my body.

"Alright." Thompson closed the notebook with a resounding snap and shoved it into his pocket and then headed for the door. "Give me a few." He paused at the door, his hand on the knob as he turned back to me. "And it was nice to meet you . . . ?"

"You can call me Zee," the demon inside of me smirked. "Muriel's better half."

I tried to roll my eyes, which was hard to do since Zee apparently had control of my facial expressions.

When Thompson was gone, Zee turned his attention to the cuffs. "Hmmm . . . should we break out or wait until someone comes back and really freak them out?"

Oh, are you talking to me?

"Of course, I'm talking to you," Zee quipped. "We have a schedule to keep, and as Asmodeus told you, I'm already behind. So, since I'm destroying your life, I thought I'd at least give you the deciding factor."

I huffed. *How generous of you.*

"I thought so too," Zee said, pulling on the cuffs slightly. "I think it would be more dramatic to wait until that guy Riley comes back. Maybe I could rip him apart before we head out. Or . . ." he pursed my lips and glanced up at the ceiling, "I could just break out and kill everyone in the other room."

You're forgetting something.

"What?" Zee cocked my head to the side. "I mean, this outfit isn't exactly the one I'd hoped to be wearing when this all went down, but it will have to do."

I held back an annoyed growl. *You're forgetting the guns.*

"Hmmm. That does pose a problem. I mean, they wouldn't kill you, but that could slow us down a little bit, especially when it comes to opening the portal to heaven. I don't want my master to punish me for damaging the goods."

I wished I had control of my head because I would bang it against the metal table over and over again. It would be better than listening to Zee debate how he was going to escape and kill everyone.

Finally having enough, I shouted in my head. *Why don't you just wait until we get out of here and then no one has to die!?*

Zee paused in his debate and clicked my tongue. "What's the fun in that?"

It would solve your problem.

"But then you will take control of your body again, and that will not do."

Before I could argue with him, the door to the room opened.

"How about this?" Zee said quickly before the person came in. "If it's Riley, I kill him and make a break for it. If it's not, then I kill everyone and make a break for it."

I didn't get the chance to answer because a person came in. To my utter relief, it was my lawyer, Patrick Mayer, and in his hands was a piping hot cup of what I hoped was the herbal tea I requested.

"Miss Wiles." Mr. Mayer smiled at me, holding the cup in his hand without offering it to me. "So good to see you again. Unfortunate that it is under such circumstances."

"Are we free to go?" Zee eagerly beamed at Mr. Mayer.

"Not just yet . . ." Mr. Mayer trailed off and then stepped out of the way of the doorway. Thompson came in behind him with two other officers. Frowning at them, Zee glanced between them. "What's this? Are we going to have a party?" Zee licked my lips. "I could get behind that, but not with you . . ." Zee gestured to Mr. Mayer. "I'm not even sure what you are."

Without warning, Thompson and the other officers pinned my body to the chair while Mr. Mayer poured the hot liquid into my mouth. Zee didn't realize what was happening until he'd already swallowed enough of it to shove him back down to where he belonged.

It all happened so fast that Zee didn't have the chance to retaliate and do any of the things he had been promising to do the whole time. It helped that I had the majority of control over my body so that any thought of attacking the officers was squashed by my will to fight. I clenched my hands into fists and pushed myself down into the chair as much as I could, using my angelic strength against him.

The others didn't release me until I gasped and blinked. Slowly lifted my hand to signal I was okay.

"Mary?" Thompson asked with a hopeful look.

"Yeah, thanks." I bobbed my head toward him and then the others. "Sorry for all the hassle."

"You gotta keep those demons down," one of the officers said.

My brows lifted. "Uh . . . yeah."

"Don't worry, Mary." Thompson patted my shoulder. "These guys were part of the crew from the warehouse shoot-out. No need to fear them telling."

I swallowed and nodded again. "Thank you. I mean it."

"Here." Mr. Mayer held the cup out to me. "I suggest you finish that before we get you out of here. It will be hard to explain how you're not a dangerous flight risk if you're trying to kill everyone."

I gave a wry smile before downing the rest of the mixture. Grimacing, I coughed. "Tastes like three-day-old ass."

Thompson chuckled and uncuffed me from the table. "I'll take your word for it."

15

"WHAT DO WE DO now?" Trisha asked as we left the precinct.

I wrapped an arm around her shoulder, knowing she needed comforting right now. "We go home and plan for the worst. Besides, Adara's lawyer said that Billie's funeral is tomorrow. We can't miss it."

"No, we can't," Trisha murmured, her head down. "Why does all this bad shit keep happening to us?"

I shrugged. "The hazards of the job, I guess."

Trisha lifted her head to look at me. "I doubt that many PIs deal with demons and death as much as we do."

I sighed. "I suppose not. Do you want to quit?"

Scoffing, Trisha pushed away from me. "And let that douchebag win? No way."

I grinned slightly. "I hoped you'd say that. I don't know what I would have done without you."

Smirking, Trisha bumped me on the shoulder with her fist. "Never would have gotten with Sid, that's for sure."

I gaped at her. "You think I can't attract a man on my own?"

Trisha giggled. "Attract one? Yes. Keep one without saying something weird and scaring him away? No way."

"Pfft, I wasn't that bad."

We smiled at each other for a long moment before my lips started to dip. "I heard the funeral is going to have a lot of celebrities. Are you sure you want to go?"

Trisha shrugged. "It's our one chance to catch Carl. It only seems right to finish what we started, you know? And besides, we owe it to Billie."

I adjusted my gun holster, happy to have it back. "I'm not sure we'd be welcome though. We are the prime suspects for her murder."

"We have to try."

Bobbing my head, I followed her to the car. The only reason we weren't getting bombarded with cameras and reporters was because the cops hadn't released any information about who they suspected to be Billie's killer. Or at least Thompson said so. They wouldn't know until they reviewed the security videos. I wasn't sure exactly what they would show, but it would be obvious that we didn't kill her. There were no bullet holes in her, and the autopsy already showed she'd died from a broken neck. A neck broken by her celebrity demon boyfriend. Whether or not anyone believed us . . . that was still to be seen since said boyfriend apparently had been MIA for quite some time.

A lot of things did not add up.

"I should call my mom." Trisha sighed and sank down in her seat. "She's probably freaking out. She was a big fan of Billie."

"Did she know we were working her case?" I started the car and pulled out of the parking lot. Trisha winced. "Trisha. You know you're not supposed to give away who we are working with unless absolutely necessary. It violates their privacy."

"Well, she's dead now." Trisha snorted, crossing her arms and shrugging her shoulders. "Moot point."

"That's beside the point."

"Have you checked in with Sid?" Trisha asked with an arched brow.

I frowned. "Why would I do that?"

"Oh, I don't know." Trisha sat up straight and leaned a hand on the dashboard as we jerked to a stop at a red light. "He's your boyfriend. You've been in lockup for three days. You almost went full-out demon on all those cops while in there. You're lucky we got the lawyer to go get the herbs when we did."

"Yeah . . ." I drew out and grimaced. "I'm not sure they believed I needed those herbs for my sickness."

Trisha huffed. "Don't make light of this. We might still have a job to do, but you also have a decision to make. You know Asmodeus wasn't kidding. If he could easily kill Billie, someone he'd been screwing for the last year, then he will just as easily kill me or worse." She shivered and rubbed her hands up and down her arms.

I reached over and placed a hand on her arm. "I won't let him touch you. I promise."

Shaking her head so that her dark hair fell around her face, Trisha murmured, "Don't make promises you might not be able to keep. Hell on Earth versus your friends has always been the worst choice in all those hero movies."

"And yet . . ." I pointed out as we pulled into the driveway of her house, "everything works out in the end, right?"

Trisha slowly lifted her head and stared at me. "This isn't fiction, Mary. Heroes don't always win. Sometimes everyone just dies."

She shoved out of the car and stormed up the driveway before I could say anything else.

I wanted to reassure her. To tell her everything would be alright. Problem was . . . I thought she might be right.

Pulling up to the office, I frowned. There were several people standing outside of my office door and not one of them looked like they actually needed my help. Not if the cameras they were trying to hide were anything to go by.

"Mary Wiles?" The first woman came up to me with a bright smile. "The private detective?"

"That's what it says on my business cards," I said, pushing through the group of people.

"So, you were working on the stalker case for Billie? Do you have anything you can tell us about her murder? Who did it? Was it her stalker, Carl? Have you found him? What did the cops say to you? Do they think you did it? Why would they think you're responsible when you were trying to keep her safe?"

I shook my head, muttering as I unlocked the door, "That's what I'd like to know," before slamming it in the reporter's faces.

I stomped up the stairs, getting a satisfying thrill with each loud thump my boots made on the steps until I reached my office door. It was actually pretty smart of the lawyer to lock the bottom entry door when he came before, or I'd have had a harder time getting to my front door. Madame Serena's old shop was still dark and boarded up from the incident, so I didn't have to worry about them poking around in there.

Opening the office door, I sighed into the darkness. Things were so much simpler when I first arrived to Earth. Sure, I didn't know as much as I did now, but as they say, ignorance is bliss. In this case, they'd been right.

I removed my holster from my shoulders, surprised the cops even gave it back to me, and sat it down on Trisha's desk. A bedazzled water bottle sat next to the computer, not something that Trisha would ever own.

Billie's. It had to be.

I picked it up and sat down on the edge of the desk, staring at it.

This wasn't the first time I'd lost someone to the enemy, and I doubted it would be the last. And while Billie was annoying, she didn't deserve to go out like that. Not because of a demon.

My fingers curled tightly around the bottle.

Not because of me.

With a wail, I threw the bottle as hard as I could against the far wall. Rage burned through me. How could I have let this happen? Why hadn't I stopped this before it had gotten this far? I swept my arm across the desk, knocking everything to the floor. What was the point of being an angel of God if I couldn't even save one young girl?

I picked up the computer monitor and lifted it over my head, breathing heavily. "What's the point?" I screamed into the dark and launched the monitor at the wall. The cords ripped from their ports and plastic cracked. The monitor fell to the floor, leaving a hole in the plaster.

Squatting down, I bent my head over my knees and took in deep breaths. What was I going to do? I grabbed the back of my head, pulling at my hair with my fists. Maybe Trisha was right. Maybe we just all died.

"Now, now, that's not the Muriel I know," a voice called out to me.

Lifting my head, I saw light fill the room, and Uriel appeared with a pensive smile.

"What do you want?" I snapped, shoving to my feet. "Did you come to gloat about how I'm in over my head? That I deserve everything that's come to me for disobeying? 'Cause if so, save it." I shoved passed Uriel. "I have nothing to say to you."

"Oh, Muriel. Have you lost so much of your faith that you would turn away help when needed?" Uriel tut-tutted.

I made her follow after me as I went to the miniature fridge. Jerking it open, I found the leftover bottle of dark alcohol Trisha had left here. Popping the top, I turned around and drank straight from the bottle, eyeballing Uriel the whole time.

Uriel sighed. "Already taking up their vices, I see. Perhaps you have truly fallen now."

I lowered the bottle and swiped a hand over my mouth. "I have done nothing of the sort." I angled my head to the side and smirked. "Just like our father."

Uriel walked around my office, picking up things from the desk before setting them back down where they belonged. "You know as well as I do our father works in mysterious ways. Just because it seems like he isn't helping you doesn't mean that's the case."

"Works in mysterious ways." I snorted, taking another drink. "Nice way of saying he helps when he wants to. Well? Where is he now? Isn't this his job? Saving the world?"

Smiling furtively, Uriel stopped before me, taking the bottle from my hands. "How do you know he didn't send you here in the first place for this very reason?"

I scowled. "Don't try and make me believe this all happened for a reason. He didn't let me chase after Ramiel or get captured by demons all for his larger plan of saving the world from Lucifer."

Uriel sniffed the top of the bottle before grimacing and saying, "Didn't he?"

I snatched the bottle back from her. "No, he didn't. So, if you'll excuse me, I have to figure out how to save my friends, keep Lucifer from getting into heaven, and still find my wings so I can get back to heaven." I turned my back on her, drinking even more than I would have normally to spite her.

"But do you?"

I spun around. "Of course, I do. I can't just leave them all to die. I'm not you."

Uriel stepped up to me and placed a hand on my shoulder, the look in her eye unsettling. "No, you are not. You're Mary Wiles, Private Detective, and you will find a way." With those final words, Uriel disappeared in a flash of light.

I lifted the bottle to my lips. Were all angels such pretentious jerks?

16

I'D NEVER BEEN TO a human funeral before. In heaven, we rarely had them. Not anymore, anyway. Back when we were constantly at war with the demons, there were funerals every other day. They were nothing like the way the humans celebrated someone's passing.

What was the point of putting the body in the ground? It would decompose anyway, and who wanted to be remembered that way? Angels burned the dead. For the dead were simply that. The bodies did not matter, only the essence inside.

I wasn't human though. So, if I got killed, I'd just be dead. Nothing. Unlike the humans, who were given an afterlife. It didn't seem fair. I suppose I understood Lucifer's hate of them in that way.

Billie's funeral was a large event. It was to be expected for how popular she was. There was far more security at Billie's funeral than there had been at her fitting. Which was ironic considering that they couldn't keep her safe.

I couldn't keep her safe.

"There's so many people," Trisha murmured next to me by the car, hiding her red eyes behind a big pair of sunglasses.

"Did you really think there wouldn't be?" I crossed my arms and searched the area, keeping an eye out for Carl, or worse, Asmodeus.

Trisha sniffed and blew her nose. "No, I'm surprised there aren't more."

I bumped her with my elbow. "That's because they're keeping the riff-raff out." I pointed to where the security guards were directing people into the graveyard area.

"How are we going to get in?" Trisha asked. "We aren't exactly the crème de la crème."

I slid my sunglasses into place and grabbed my PI badge and gun. "Leave that to me. Billie might have died on my watch, but I wouldn't leave her case unfinished, and if Carl is going to show anywhere, it's going to be here to honor his obsession."

We climbed out of the car and headed toward the checkpoint where large men in black suits and sunglasses were checking people off a list as if it were the biggest event of the season.

"Name?" the first security guard asked.

I glanced at Trisha and then back to the guard. "Mary Wiles and Trisha Larsen."

"I don't have you on the list. I'm afraid you'll have to wait behind the line with the rest of the . . . fans." The guard waved his hand over the group of sobbing individuals, mostly women.

"Actually," I turned away from the fans and back to the guard, "we were working for

Billie when she passed. We have a contract to uphold to apprehend her stalker."

The guard snorted. "Fat lot of good it did. She's still dead."

"Excuse me!" Trisha cried out, shaking her fist at the guard. "How dare you speak about Billie that way? She was a dear friend of mine."

"Then why isn't your name on the list?" The guard tapped it with a sneer.

"Trisha?" A woman's voice called out. "Trisha Larsen."

Trisha tried to look around the large man to the woman calling her name. "Yes. It's me, Mrs. Noff. Trisha Larsen."

A petite woman with bleached blonde hair the same shade as Billie's shoved between the two large guards. "Get out of the way, you buffoons. These are my daughter's close friends."

"But ma'am, they aren't on the list." The guard held the clipboard up as if it was all-knowing.

"Neither is the pope, and he's here, isn't he?!" She turned and waved a hand at an elderly man with a white cap. "Now let them in."

The guards exchanged a look before reluctantly stepping aside to let us pass. I followed after Trisha, who had been scooped up by Billie's mother and was being led to the front of the group.

"I can't believe the police thought you had anything to do with Billie's death." Mrs. Noff shook her head and sniffed politely. "It was that Carl Kauffman; I just know it."

"Yeah . . ." Trisha drew out looking over her shoulder at me. "I'm sure it was. That's why Mary is here. She's sure he's going to show up."

Mrs. Noff gasped and placed her hands on the sides of her face. "Do you really think he'll show up?"

I nodded and jerked my head toward the casket. "Oh, he'll show. If he's even half as much of a crazed fan as those people, then we can no doubt expect a special appearance from Carl."

Sniffing once more, Mrs. Noff nodded slightly. "Oh yes, then he will certainly come. Billie never let us know how much she and

Carl talked, but from what I understand, he was deeply involved in her career."

I placed a hand on her shoulder, giving her the reassurance she obviously needed. "Don't worry. I'll get him. Just focus on Billie today. She wouldn't want you to worry."

She gave me a grateful smile before turning to Trisha. "Will you sit with me? She would have wanted someone who knew her before all this at the front."

"Of course." Trisha wrapped her arm around Mrs. Noff's shoulders and then asked me, "Will you be okay?"

I lowered my glasses to look around. "Yeah. I'll be good as long as you-know-who doesn't show up."

"God willing," Trisha muttered and led Mrs. Noff to the front.

I stood in the back, my arms crossed, and my eyes scanning the area. I didn't want Carl or anyone else to get the drop on us. I briefly wished Adara had come to help me keep watch, but after calling in the favor to the guild's lawyer, she had been "persuaded" to come back and talk things over. I wasn't sure how much talking there would actually be.

Adara wasn't known to be the forgive-and-forget type.

The funeral began shortly after we arrived. Everyone quieted except the reporters that were off to one side and allowed to report on the day's events from a distance. A man I didn't know stood up behind the podium next to Billie's picture and casket.

"Today we are here to not mourn but to celebrate the life of one of the best people I have ever had the pleasure of meeting. Billie Noff." There was a pause as he allowed the crowd to cry and coo in turn. He continued on to talk about Billie as if she were an angel sent from heaven. I tuned most of it out as I kept watch.

So far, so good. No Carl and most definitely no Asmodeus. If luck was on our side, then today would be uneventful. Unfortunately, in my experience, that never happens.

It would do everyone good to catch Carl now rather than later. The family needed peace of mind, and if I was being honest, I needed to catch him to assuage the guilt I felt about Billie's death.

My head turned slowly as if on a dial as I skimmed the crowd. There were lots of large hats and even larger sunglasses. It seemed everyone was coming out to be seen rather than to say goodbye to Billie.

One man stood out in the crowd of seated individuals. I was no expert in what made something in fashion or not but this one had a different feeling than the rest. He didn't sit quite as proudly. Didn't shine quite as much as the rest of the celebrity guests. In fact, besides Trisha and Billie's mother, he seemed to be the only one who was distressed by the event.

If only I could see his face.

Inching around the back of the crowd, I made my way toward the man. He wore a hat and sunglasses making it harder to identify him from the back or side. I couldn't tell much about his build beneath the suit from where I stood, but he seemed like he could be the right size for Carl. Asmodeus was quite a bit smaller and would never slouch in such a manner as he did.

When Billie's mother stood up, she pulled Trisha up with her, clutching her arm tightly as if she would fall if she wasn't there. This made the man look up from his hands. His jaw clenched, and he straightened in his seat.

Who was he upset at? Trisha? The mother? I couldn't tell.

I kept my eyes on him and tried to get closer, but the onlookers hanging out around the back were making it impossible to get through.

When I finally made it passed the horde, he was gone. My head jerked from side to side, searching, searching. Where had he gone?

Not knowing where Carl had gone, I chose to go for his target instead.

I headed toward the front to many people's protests. Before I reached them, Carl stepped out from behind the large flower arrangement, tears pouring down his face and a gun in his hand.

"You shouldn't be here," he cried out, his gun firmly pointed at Trisha. The crowd cried out in terror, and Carl swept the gun around.

"Nobody moves." He pointed the gun back at Trisha. "You were supposed to be protecting her, and now she's gone. If you hadn't gotten in the way, I would have taken her away from all this."

"Carl," Mrs. Noff tried to reason with him. "Billie wouldn't want this."

"You don't know what she wanted," Carl yelled. "You never did. That's why she confided in me." He slapped his free hand on his chest. "I was the only one who understood her, and you," he jerked his gun at Trisha, "you took her away from me."

Trying to not draw Carl's attention, I moved around the back of the flowers, drawing my gun. If the security guards couldn't get here in time, then it might be up to me to step in. I wouldn't let Trisha get hurt. Not again.

Trisha stayed where she was, her hands up in front of her. "Carl, I didn't kill Billie. You can ask the police."

Carl barked a laugh. "Those idiots can't even solve the cases they have. I've never trusted them to do what was right. But I will . . ." He placed both hands on his gun just as the security guards came sweeping in.

I jumped toward Trisha as the guards tackled Carl. The gun went off, and pain ripped through my chest.

"Mary," Trisha cried out as I hit the ground. "Are you okay?" The people around us began screaming and running away, no one caring about the person that was actually injured. "Can I get some help over here?!"

I groaned and tried not to move. "Why am I always the one who gets shot?"

THE BEEPING OF THE heart monitor woke me. I shifted in the hospital bed and winced. Nope, still hurts.

Why did I jump in front of the bullet again? I might be an angel, but I still could die just the same.

"Mary?" A small hand clasped mine.

Oh, yeah. Trisha.

I cracked my eyes open a slit to see her. Her face was clear of makeup for the first time ever. "Your face looks weird," I tried to say, but my mouth wasn't working right.

"Oh, here." Trisha grabbed a cup off the side table and offered the straw to me. "Water."

I tilted my head up and sipped through the straw, the cool water coating my burning throat. "Thanks."

"Of course. You saved my life . . . again." Trisha huffed a laugh and set the cup down. "What were you trying to say?"

Licking my lips, I jerked my head toward her face. "Your face looks weird like that."

Trisha touched her face and then dropped her hand with a scowl. "Well, all the crying at the funeral and then thinking I'd finally killed you made my makeup into a big mess of racoon eyes. I just washed the whole thing off rather than deal with it."

My lips curled up slightly.

"What?" Trisha asked.

I reached a hand weakly out toward her. "You washed your face for me."

Trisha ducked out of reach. "Yeah, well, don't get used to it. You can only jump in front of bullets for me so many times before you die."

I snorted and shifted in the bed. "Let's hope there's no more bullets to block in the future."

"I hope so." Trisha sighed and then touched my hand. "Does it hurt? Do I need to call the nurse?"

I shook my head and squeezed her hand. "No, it's alright. I don't want to be under too many drugs. We still have Zee to worry about."

"Oh god!" Trisha gasped bringing her hand to her mouth. "I forgot about Zee."

I frowned, my brows furrowing. "What about him? He's not talking right now, so maybe whatever they gave me is keeping him quiet." I lifted the hand with an IV in it.

"But you haven't taken any herbs in over a day. Didn't Octavia say that it would stop working after a while?"

I shrugged. "Like I said, the hospital seems to have pushed him down with whatever drugs are pumping through this."

Trisha frowned and walked toward the door. "I'd still feel better if you took the tea anyway. I'm just going to go get it. Don't go anywhere."

I lifted my hands with a small smile. "Where am I going to go?"

As Trisha left, Thompson walked in. "Miss Larsen."

"I think we've known each other long enough that you can call me Trisha, Sergeant."

"And you can call me Randall." He paused and then cleared his throat. "Or Thompson."

Trisha smiled awkwardly. "Yeah, Thompson is fine. Can you keep an eye on Mary? I need to get her special medicine."

Thompson glanced from Trisha to me with a nod. "Of course. I need to speak with Wiles anyway."

"Just a warning, she's still kind of out of it from the drugs," Trisha told him and then waved goodbye, closing the door behind her.

Thompson walked toward the bed and sat in the chair next to me. "So, you're riding that morphine high, huh?"

My head lulled to the side. "Is that what it is?"

Smiling at me, Thompson leaned back in his chair. "You know, a while ago, you weren't even affected by the pain medicine. They had to keep upping your dose because your body burned it off so fast. And now here you are . . ."

"Here I am." I lifted my hand and then winced. "Ouch."

Thompson watched me carefully. "Why is that?"

"Why is what?" I asked, smacking my lips together. They felt funny. In fact, everything felt good. So good. I should do this medicine thing more often.

"Why are you more affected now than before?"

My shoulders did a weird floopy thing that I think was supposed to be a shrug. "Probably 'cause I'm losing more of my powers."

Thompson's brows bunched together. "And is that normal?"

"Hey." I pointed at him with a serious tone. "I'm an angel without her wings stuck on Earth. I blew my load." I paused to chuckle slightly at that. "Blew my load . . .

anyway, I used a lot of power to try and kill Asmodeus and ended up killing my commanding officer instead."

"So, what does that mean?" Thompson leaned forward, his hands laced before him.

"If I don't get my wings?"

"Yes."

I shifted my head to the side, not looking at Thompson, the thought starting to sober me slightly. "If I don't get my wings back, I'll eventually become human. Or basically human. No soul, remember?"

"That seems kind of cruel."

I jerked my head back to Thompson and instantly regretted it. "Did you think God was anything but?"

"For someone who hates God and all the angels, you have seemed pretty hell-bent—for lack of a better word—on getting back there," Thompson pointed out with a pensive look.

I pushed the button on the bed, slowly lifted the head of my bed. Once I was able to look Thompson straight in the eye, though it pained me to do it, I stopped. "The longer I've been away, the more time I have had to see the faults. And I don't hate them per se . . ." I blew out a heavy breath, ". . . I just don't know how to trust any of them again after what happened."

"Then why don't you stay?"

I scoffed. "Stay? I can't stay. I don't belong here. Look at all the chaos I've caused."

"I don't know about that . . ." Thompson began.

"Look at all the death that's happened because of me. And you . . . you wouldn't have had to deal with any of this stuff had I not been around." I jerked my hand toward him, forgetting I had an IV in. "Fuck. And then Trisha wouldn't have gotten hurt so many times. She'd be doing something safe like a desk job for some security firm. Or whatever."

"And do you think we'd be happier not knowing?" Thompson angled his head to the side, watching me. "While I have seen and learned a lot of stuff I never in my wildest nightmares expected to ever know, I wouldn't give it up to be in the dark again. And I don't know about Trisha, but I don't think she would want to go back to boring IT work. She loves you, and we would all miss you."

"I guess." I sighed, chewing on my lower lip. "I just don't see how me staying would be good for anyone."

"Don't you have a boyfriend now?" Thompson reminded me, lifting his brows. "Do you think he wants you to go?"

"Look." I cut him off with a slice of my hand. "This is all hypothetical anyway. I have to actually find my wings before it even matters. Let's just focus on the problem at hand."

"And what's that?"

"Getting this demon out of me and then stopping the freaking apocalypse," I explained and then had a thought. "Are we still the lead suspects for Billie's death?"

Thompson shook his head. "The security cameras came back from the scene and proved what you were all saying. So now that actor—Dash—is number one on our wanted list, but apparently no one knows where to find him. He's been MIA for months now."

I huffed. "Good luck finding him. Asmodeus only shows up when he wants to be found."

"What will make him want to be found?"

"Me."

Thompson frowned. "What do you mean?" His eyes widened. "No. We're not using you as bait."

"Why not?" I shrugged. "It's after the funeral. He's going to be coming for my answer anyway. Might as well make it worth it."

Thompson stroked his jawline and stared at nothing. "That might work, but how are we going to trap him? Take him out? Hey, do you have any more of those holy bullets? I could get a squad ready, and we could do it like we did at the warehouse."

"I can get some more made," I told him, getting excited to finally take Asmodeus down. "You know . . ." My lips slowly curled up into a smile. "We could even put all those murders on him too. Or the actor he's been riding. No doubt that poor guy has already been smoked out."

"Really?"

"Oh yeah." I inclined my head. "Asmodeus has been riding him for long enough that there's no way that guy is still in there. Plus, Asmodeus is a demon lord. A high-level demon who wouldn't bother keeping a soul in its body for longer than he needed."

Thompson pushed up from his seat and pulled his phone out. "I have a good feeling about this, Wiles. We can finally get our guys."

I saluted him. "One can hope."

"Rest up." Thompson pointed at me and then added on, "Maybe pump up the morphine until Trisha comes back with your special medicine."

I lifted my hand, giving him a thumbs-up. "Good idea. I was starting to feel a bit too clear-headed."

I pushed the button that gave me more medicine as Thompson left. I felt the medicine begin to work again instantly. My eyes grew heavy, and my head bobbed. I guess it wouldn't hurt to sleep just a little bit. At least, until Trisha gets back.

18

THE FIRST THING I noticed when my mind started to wake back up was the ache in my chest. Then the fact that my butt was not on a nice and cushy hospital bed but on a hard seat.

"I'm sorry to pull you from your recovery bed so soon," A smooth velvety voice commented from a few feet away.

Rolling my shoulders, my eyes flickered open and landed on the wooden table before me. This wasn't the hospital. Where was I?

"Do you need something for the pain?" the voice asked, drawing my attention up from the table and into the piercing blue eyes of Lucifer. "I hear you have become more human since you've lost your wings." He winced and rubbed his hands together before him. "That must have been painful."

I rolled my jaw, stretching it out. "Excruciating."

"I can imagine." Lucifer nodded, rolling up the sleeves of his black button-down shirt. For someone who'd been stuck in hell for so long, he sure had a fix on the fashion on Earth.

Maybe he was getting tips from the demons? Why was I even thinking about that? Trisha was rubbing off on me too much.

"What am I doing here, and where is here?" I shifted in my seat, realizing I hadn't been tied up. Things were looking up.

Lucifer lifted his hands and smiled. "You don't recognize it?"

I turned my head slowly to look around the room. The place seemed familiar, but the pain in my chest made it impossible to figure out what exactly I was seeing.

"Let me help you out." Lucifer stepped around the table and walked toward me, sliding his fingers along the surface. "I was standing just about here, and you were . . ." He pointed a few steps away from him. "I believe astral projecting?"

"Oh, got it." I inclined my head. "So, why am I here?"

Lucifer sat on the edge of the table, too close to me for comfort. "I believe Asmodeus told you what I wanted."

Asmodeus. The sound of the demon lord's name made me straighten. Thompson and I made a plan. What was going to happen when I wasn't there?

"Oh, don't worry about your policeman friend." Lucifer answered the question I hadn't voiced. "Asmodeus already jumped bodies and left that actor person for your friend to capture." He chuckled. "Lucky that guy's soul was already gone, or he'd be up on so many murders. But you know . . . we know who really committed those murders, don't we?"

"Why would you do that?"

Lucifer reached out and tipped my chin in his hand. "I can't have my favorite angel distracted now, can I? We have work to do, and if you're thinking about those filthy apes on Earth, then you won't be focused on the task at hand."

I tried to pull my face away from him, but it seemed that Zee still had partial control of my body. "And what exactly would I be focusing on?" I knew what Lucifer wanted from me, but I needed him to keep talking so I could figure out a way out of this. Somehow.

"Don't play coy." Lucifer shook his finger at me. "You know exactly what I want from you, Muriel."

"You're an archangel. Just do it yourself." I struggled to move out of the chair and scowled when I barely moved an inch.

Lucifer sighed and stood from the table, rubbing his temples with one hand. "You know I can't do that. Even with Michael's dagger, I can't cut the fabric of time and space. I'm a fallen angel. Only a nonfallen one, still in God's favor, can make a portal to heaven."

I snorted. "Well, I'm hardly in God's favor, and I'm not exactly up to full angel powers, you know. I wasted a lot of that on Ramiel."

"Yes, yes, yes." Lucifer waved me off. "I know about all that. But once you have your wings back, you'll be restored to full power and will have the power to get me what I want."

I stared at him for a long moment and then asked, "What makes you think I won't turn on you the moment I have my wings back? Zee won't be able to hold me once I'm at full power. In fact, you're basically signing his death warrant by giving me my wings." I was hoping the demon in question would realize the suicide mission his master had put him on and let me go.

Lucifer smirked. "You think my followers don't know what they're signing up for? Zee knew what was going to happen the whole time. In fact, he was counting on it."

"Why?" I gaped at him. "Why would he sign up for something that would get him killed?"

Shrugging nonchalantly, a self-satisfied grin on his face, Lucifer held his hands out to either side. "To see the glory of hell brought down on those who have opposed us, of course. The ends justify the means and all that." He waved his hand in the air briefly. "Now, what makes me think you'll do what I ask once you have your full powers?"

I didn't answer him, my previous plan shot.

"I know you'll do what I want, or I will have Asmodeus kill every single one of your friends on Earth. Slowly and painfully until you comply. Then, when that doesn't work, I will put you back in that room."

I tried not to flinch, but it was a lost cause.

"Oh yes, I know about that. I know everything that goes on in my world. I, after all, created it." Lucifer's lip curled up maliciously. "I'll have your wings removed and then reattached over and over again. Until you do what I want."

Bile built up in my throat, and I swallowed it down, gasping, "What about the blade? I don't even have it on me."

Lucifer tut-tutted. "Now, that's not exactly true, is it?"

My body moved on its own as I reached down and shoved my pant leg up, withdrawing the very blade this whole thing had been about.

"You were saying?"

Where had that come from? How had I not known it was even there?

Zee chuckled in my head. *Trisha isn't as good at hiding things as you thought. Burying it in the park...really?*

The dirt in my nails from before! That's where that had come from. I wanted to smack myself for being too slow to see it before but my arms weren't in my control.

Placing the blade on the table before me, I weighed my options. There weren't any. Not that I could see right then, anyway. The only choice I had was to do what Lucifer wanted and rain hell down on heaven and in turn, Earth. Did I sacrifice my friends and myself for everyone else? Or did I sacrifice those who had turned their back on me when I chased after Ramiel?

Lifting my eyes from the table, I locked my gaze with Lucifer's. "I'll do it."

"Ah." Lucifer clapped his hands gleefully. "I knew you would come around to my way of thinking."

"But," I stopped him from patting himself on the back even more, "I want something else in return."

Lucifer's lips turned down, and he cocked his head to the side. "I honestly hadn't expected a negotiation, but sure . . ." He pulled a chair out from the table and sat down, crossing one leg over the other. "Go ahead with your demands."

"There's just one," I stated with a viciousness that surprised even me. "I want Asmodeus."

"Asmodeus?" Lucifer's eyes lit up. "I knew you had a thing for his spawn, but I never thought you'd want the beast himself."

"Ew." My nose scrunched up at the thought. "I want him dead. Gone. Never to see the light of day."

Lucifer hummed. "That's quite a big ask. He is one of my top generals. Why?"

"I want to make sure he leaves everyone else alone back on Earth. He made some promises to some friends of mine that I don't intend to allow him to keep, and this way, everyone wins."

"Except Asmodeus."

I shrugged or tried to. "As you said once, sacrifices have to be made for the survival of us all."

Lucifer looked positively overjoyed that I'd remembered what he'd said all those eons ago. Not like it was easy to forget. He was the cautionary tale that kept all the other little angels in line.

"Alright." Lucifer knocked his fist on the table. "I'll do it. Or rather, you can do it. You are the one who wants him dead, after all. But first," he shoved away from the table and offered me his hand, "Let's get you your wings back."

19

ZEE ALLOWED ME TO walk on my own. Probably because he realized I had no choice in the matter. There was nothing I could do. No way out of this situation that I could see. There was no way but to go along with Lucifer to keep all my people safe.

Lucifer led me to another room where my wings hung inside of a glass box. The shimmering white feathers fluttered at my presence, wanting to be reunited as much as I wanted them too. I moved toward the box and placed a hand on the glass, so close and yet so far away from the thing I wanted most in this world. Or at least, it *was* the thing I wanted most. I wasn't so sure anymore.

"Now, it will be just as painful to reattach them as it was to remove them," Lucifer warned me, stepping up next to me. "I want to prepare you for it. This isn't the first pair of wings I've had to reattach." His hand rubbed his shoulder and upper back as if it had been he that had his wings put back on.

I glanced away from my wings and turned to him. "I'm ready."

Lucifer inclined his head and walked around the case. Pulling a key from his pocket, he unlocked the case and flung the doors wide open. I thought he would be the one to put them back on me, but the moment they were free, the wings shot out of the case, nearly knocking Lucifer down in their race to get to me. I barely had time to brace myself before they slammed into my back.

A searing pain unlike anything I'd felt before burned through my back and down my spine. My hands hit the glass before me, shattering it on contact as I screamed out my agony. Lucifer hadn't been lying. It was as if I were reliving the torture of having my wings removed the first time but ten times worse. The pain was never-ending, or at least felt like it, until I found myself blinking and gasping on the stone floor.

"Alright there?" Lucifer knelt beside me, peering over me.

I swallowed down a witty comeback and pushed up to my knees, something that was easier now that I had my wings attached. It was as if until now, I had been walking with one eye closed the entire time. Everything was straighter, easier.

"Much better, huh?" Lucifer offered me a hand, and while I loathed to take it, I had to keep up the charade.

"Yes." I moved my wings slowly, testing them, one and then the other. "It's strange."

"I can imagine," Lucifer commented, watching me move my newly found wings. "To lose a piece of yourself. It's almost worse than dying. It must be nice to have it back now."

I nodded, not knowing what to say. I did know what I was going to do next, though.

With my wings came a jolt of celestial power. All the energy I had wasted on trying to kill Asmodeus came back in a rush that almost gave me a power high. And I knew exactly what I was going to do with my new power. Gathering up my celestial aura, I shoved it through every pore of my body, cleaning out any dark spots and impurities, which included Zee. He disintegrated without so much as a sound, and then I was back to being my pure angelic self.

"Feel better?" Lucifer angled his head to the side with a knowing smile.

"Much."

"Now, for your part." Lucifer swept an arm back toward the other room where the blade still sat on the table. Someone else I didn't know sat at the table as well. The man stood at our entry. A familiar smile on his lips.

"My lord." The man bowed to Lucifer. "I see all is going as planned."

"Yes, Asmodeus, despite your efforts." Lucifer dismissed him with a flick of his eyes over to me. "Muriel has proven to be most cooperative."

"I am pleased." Asmodeus nodded and then frowned. "Though, I would caution you, my lord. This one is not to be trusted."

"Do you think I was born yesterday?" Lucifer snapped at Asmodeus and snatched up the blade from the table. "That I would be so easily tricked?"

"No, no." Asmodeus held his hands up and backed up a step. "Of course not, my lord. I just simply know how Muriel works."

"And I do not?" Lucifer snarled, turning to me. "I have known her since the dawn of time. Do not think you would know more than me. Now, Muriel . . ." Lucifer handed me the blade. "You will fulfill your part of the bargain, and then you may have him." He jerked his head toward Asmodeus, who blinked rapidly at him.

"Wait, what? That wasn't part of the deal," Asmodeus cried out, his face morphing into pure rage. "I have done everything you have asked and more, my lord, and you would give me over to this, this angel whore?"

"Silence." Lucifer snapped, jerking a hand at Asmodeus, causing him to freeze up in place. "You were created for my pleasure, and I will do with you as I will. If I wish to trade your life for a sandwich, then I will. Now in this case, I am trading your life for something so much more. So, take solace in knowing you have made my return to heaven possible."

Asmodeus eyes screamed even though his mouth couldn't move, and I almost felt sorry for the demon. Except . . . I didn't. He deserved everything he got and more. Including what I was going to do to him after all this was done.

"Now, Muriel . . ." Lucifer turned to me with an impatient frown. "If you please."

I sucked in a breath and flipped the blade over in my hand. "I'm not exactly sure how this works . . ."

Lucifer came up behind me, his mouth close to my ear so I could feel his breath on it. "Just think of the place you want to go. Where in the garrison would no one go? Somewhere that I could sneak into, and no one would ever know I was there. That is where I will infiltrate the heavens."

My brows furrowed as I thought about what he said, and then my brows shot up in realization. "Got it. Stand back."

Lucifer stepped away from me as I lifted my arm and slashed at the air before me. A rip of light opened up from nothing, nearly blinding me.

"At long last," Lucifer gasped, pushing up next to me. "I'll finally get to go home."

So focused on the pathway before him, Lucifer didn't notice how I tensed and stepped further away from the portal with each step forward he took. My eyes shifted over to Asmodeus, who hadn't missed the look on my face and was trying to make himself move to warn his lord. It was too late though. For both of them.

Lucifer stepped through the portal, and I quickly swiped the dagger again, closing it behind him.

"You did not send him to heaven," Asmodeus breathed out with a snarl, finally able to move again now that Lucifer was not in the same room as him. He wasn't even on the same plane anymore.

I shrugged. "Hey, it's not my fault he didn't specify which part of heaven he wanted to go to."

"Where did you send him?" Asmodeus stalked toward me, pure fury in his face.

I flipped the blade over in my hand and grinned. "Oh, I sent him to heaven, alright, but right in the middle of a horde of cherubim."

Asmodeus gaped at me. "They'll tear him apart and then send him back down here faster than you can say Armageddon."

"Then next time, he should be more specific," I told him and lifted a hand, gathering my celestial power into my hand until a big ball of light filled the room. "You, however, will not be there to see it."

20

WALKING INTO THE NIGHT Owl for what would be one of the last times, I thought back to when I first came here.

I'd come across it accidentally. Tailing a demon that had been killing little kids in the park. I had tracked him to this very bar where I met . . . Sidney Maximus. A half-demon bartender who I'd one day fall in love with.

That very man stood behind the bar now, scribbling in a notebook. Since it was before open hours, I had him and the place all to myself. Just how I liked it.

"Knock, knock," I said, causing him to lift his head from his work and smile at me. I would miss that smile. Those eyes. Everything about him, really.

"Hey," he murmured, tucking the pen he had been writing with behind his ear. "How are you feeling? I would have come visit you in the hospital but . . ."

I grinned. "I got kidnapped by the demon riding my body?" I shrugged. "Yeah, it happens. I won't hold it against you."

Sid mock wiped his brow. "That's a load off." He leaned across the bar once I was close enough to him. I met him in the middle, pressing my lips to his in a chaste but electrifying kiss. Releasing me, Sid stayed those few inches away from my face. "Not that I'm not pleased to see you, but to what do I owe this pleasure?"

I shrugged a shoulder. "Was feeling nostalgic and wanted to come by and show you . . . these." I popped my wings out proudly, letting him soak them in.

Lifting a hand, Sid trailed his fingers down the side of the feathers. A shudder of pleasure ran through me. "Is it weird that I'm so turned on by these?"

I lowered them but didn't put them away. "No, because it's a part of me. Just like your demon half is a part of you."

Sid lowered his hand and his gaze. "That's different."

Reaching out to grab his hand before he could pull away from me, I squeezed it lightly. "No, it's not. Something I learned from having Zee inside of me all this time, fighting to get to the surface. The more you fight them, the harder it becomes, and every time he got to the surface, he had that much more control over me. I believe it's the same with you."

"What do you mean?" Sid asked, finally lifting his gaze once more.

"I mean . . ." I placed my other hand on the one with the rosary. "That maybe you need to let your other half out more than just to feed."

"What?" Sid jerked back from me. "No way. That's crazy."

"Just hear me out," I continued, following him to the back room as he tried to run away from me. "You feed him just enough to keep him down, right? What if you let him out . . . on purpose? Let him feed and get all these urges out? Then he wouldn't constantly be fighting to get out, and when he did get out, it wouldn't be as destructive as before."

Sid spun around once we were in the office. "Let me get this straight. You want me to purposely let the demon half of me out? And where would I do this? Who would be the one who suffered for it?"

"Me," I stated, making his eyes widen.

"I'd never release him on you on purpose, you know that."

I shrugged a shoulder. "I don't know. He and I have had a good time the last few times he was released, and now that I'm full angel again, it's not like he can really hurt me."

Sid stared at me for a long moment before sighing and running a hand through his hair. "I've heard worse plans. I mean, it couldn't hurt to try."

I walked toward him and wrapped my arms around his waist, placing my head on his chest. "I just want you to love all of you like I do."

Kissing the top of my head, Sid embraced me back. "And I do, Mary Wiles. Muriel. I love every part of you. Even the part that can destroy me."

On the way back to the office, I stopped at the park. I didn't know why. It wasn't like I had special feelings about this park. I did once exorcise a demon here, but that didn't make it special.

Not questioning it, I walked down the path, letting the sunshine down on me as I took in the trees and people walking by. It really was a nice park. I didn't know why I hadn't come there more often.

I moved around the park a while longer, just enjoying my time on Earth. After all, I didn't have much time left here. My lips turned down at the thought.

Stopping at a bench, I sank down on it next to an elderly man who seemed to be taking a nap.

Why did I feel so reluctant to return to heaven? This was everything I ever wanted. Everything I'd been working toward. This was it! I'd won, saved the day, beaten the bad guy, gotten my wings back. I should be happy. Ready.

And yet . . .

I didn't want to go.

"Then don't."

My head jerked toward the old man who wasn't sleeping now. "What?"

"If you don't want to go, don't." He smiled at me, the sides of his eyes crinkling.

"I didn't say that out loud," I told him, my shoulders tensing.

The old man shrugged. "You were thinking it very loudly. I couldn't help but overhear."

Not relaxing, I turned to him with a wary frown. "What are you, psychic?"

Giving me a mysterious look, the old man said, "Not in the same sense. But as an outsider to your situation. It seems that you have the answer you are looking for."

Sighing, I tilted my head down to stare at my hands. "It's not so simple. I can't just stay because I want to. I don't belong here."

"Who's to say you don't?" the old man continued, tapping his cane on the ground. "Does God decide who we love? Where we belong? Does he not give us a choice?"

"Humans, maybe." I snorted and then gave him a sideways look. "I'd never had the pleasure."

His lips pressed into a tight smile. "Of course, you have. You chose to chase after Ramiel, didn't you?"

"Well, yeah . . ."

"And you chose to fight for the humans even when you had nothing to gain from it. You were even hurt multiple times saving a few of them." He tapped his cane against the side of my leg. "Did God make you do that?"

I scowled. "No, of course not. But I'm . . . I'm an angel. I belong in heaven."

"Do you?" He arched a gray brow at me. "Because it seems to me you are exactly where you belong."

I hated to admit it, but the old man was making a lot of sense. Everyone had been telling me the same thing all along, and it took now—a complete stranger—for me to finally see it.

The old man pushed up off the bench and took a few steps away.

"Wait a minute." I stood with him, reaching out to him. "How do I know I'm making the right choice?"

He turned toward me, his cane in both hands as he grinned. "How do we know anything is the right choice? Look at me." He glanced around the park. "I didn't know the humans would be how they are today until I tried."

My brows furrowed, and then my mouth gaped open. "Fa . . . father?"

The old man tipped his hat and smiled kindly. "I did not make this world to suffer alone. They need someone to watch over them, and that person seems to be you, Muriel."

I stepped toward him. "Are you saying I can stay?"

"I'm saying do whatever makes you happiest. That's all a father ever wants for his child, isn't it?" The old man then turned and walked away. My eyes couldn't follow him, and yet he didn't disappear into the crowd.

God really was mysterious in his ways and even more so in his answers. I guess I finally had mine.

Standing on the roof of our building, I stared at the LA sunset. Nothing in heaven was quite as beautiful as the sight. Not the crystal sea. Not the rose palace. Just one of the million things about Earth that I would miss.

"They don't have those in heaven, do they?" Trisha asked, walking up behind me. "You're going to miss it. And not to forget Lou's. They don't have Chinese food there either. Or do they?"

I smiled at her, tucking my hands into my pockets. "No, they don't."

"Alcohol," Trisha added, standing next to me on the edge. "They don't have alcohol in heaven."

I snorted. "To be fair. It wouldn't do anything to any of us anyway."

"Why wouldn't they just make something stronger that would affect you?"

I chuckled and wrapped an arm around Trisha's shoulders. "Oh, Trisha. It's heaven. We're not supposed to get drunk. We're already drunk on God's presence and our divine mission."

"Blech." Trisha wrinkled her nose. "Sounds utterly boring. Remind me to not sign up for that."

Squeezing her shoulder, I leaned into her. "Believe me, it's better than the alternative."

Trisha shrugged and stepped away from me. "That's it then. I'm just never going to die."

I grinned at her. "Oh yeah? Planning on becoming immortal?"

"Yep." Trisha bobbed her head, kicking her foot against the ground. "I hear there's plenty of new things to try out in alchemy. Then there's also the fountain of youth. All kinds of other stuff. I'm sure one of them will work out."

I didn't have the heart to burst her bubble and ask her what her backup plan was. "Well, I guess I won't get to see you in heaven then."

Trisha frowned and eyeballed the ground. "Can't you come visit?"

I shook my head. "It's pretty frowned upon to come down to Earth when you're not assigned to do so. I'm afraid if I go back, I won't be able to come to visit."

Sighing dramatically, Trisha dropped her hands. "Fine. I guess I'll die and go to heaven so you won't be lonely without me."

I grinned. "You're so generous."

"Can I at least see your wings one last time?" Trisha gestured toward me with a reluctant sigh.

I arched a brow. "Why would you want to see those?"

"Well, I'm sure they look awesome on you 'cause you're, you know, awesome, and besides, when am I ever going to get to see a real live angel?"

"Uh . . . every day for the last five years?" I reminded her with a chuckle.

Trisha grunted and stomped her foot. "You know what I mean. Full-winged angel. Whatever."

"And I'm afraid you're going to have to wait a little longer for that." I moved my head from side to side, waiting for Trisha to figure it out.

Her brows furrowed, and her lips puffed out in a pout. "Why? I might not get another chance to see them. You're going to disappear one day, and then it'll be over. I don't know what I'm going to do without you." She suddenly hugged me around the middle. "Don't go. I need you. We need you. Don't make me go work for the man. I won't survive!"

I grinned down at Trisha, holding back my laughter as I patted her head. "I'm not sure who the man is, but I'm sure they would be lucky to have you. Unfortunately, they're going to have to get in line 'cause I'm not done with you yet."

"Wait, what?" Trisha lifted her head from my chest. "What do you mean? I can't assist you from heaven. I mean, do you even get cell reception up there?"

Placing my hands on Trisha's shoulders, I pushed her back slightly. "Trisha, I'm not leaving."

She blinked at me for a minute and then repeated what I said. "Well, yeah, I know you're not leaving yet, but you will eventually, and I want to be prepared for that day."

I shook my head. "No, Trisha. I'm not leaving . . . ever."

"But . . . but your wings." Trisha looked over me with wide eyes. "Your whole goal was to get your wings and go back to heaven. Well, you got your wings . . ."

"And yet . . ." I crossed my arms over my chest and looked into the distance. "I have everything I need here. I don't need my wings to get back home." I slowly smiled and lowered my eyes back down to the young woman before me. The one who had been with me through so much while I was on Earth. "I'm already there."

Trisha stared at me for a long moment, and then let out an ear-piercing squeal and grabbed a hold of me, bouncing up and down in place. "Oh my god, oh my god, oh my god! Wait, wait." She pushed me away quickly. "Wait. I just want to make sure. You aren't going back to heaven? You're going to stay here on Earth?"

I nodded. "Yes."

"And what about your wings?" Trisha peered at my shoulders as if they would sprout at any moment.

I shrugged. "I can't really get rid of them now that they're on again. So, I guess I'm officially . . . fallen."

"Nope, nope." Trisha shook her head. "No way. Fallen is for bad guys. You're . . . upgraded? Transferred? No, that's not right either." She tapped her chin and scowled. "I'm going to get this. Leave it to me."

"I will." I laughed, placing a hand on her shoulder. "What would I do without you?"

"Be bored out of your mind in heaven, duh."

Check out Her Cross To Bear!

Everything that goes bump in the night is true and they are coming for you.

With one living older brother, I thought that I would be in the clear of having to take over the family business. I could play pretend in the human world and none would be the wiser.

Until I find out my brother has gone missing and now, I was the sole heir to the Van Helsing clan!

What must my father be thinking?

I'd never been proficient at the game of masks. I tended to talk better with my fists than my mouth and I wasn't about to hold back from telling the supernatural community what was on my mind.

That's if I could live long enough to do it.

Excerpt

"Could you really kill me, pet? Put a bullet straight through my undead heart?" Xavier placed his hands over his heart his eyes watching me with curious intent.

He didn't think I'd do it.

My voice was steady and cold when I answered. "Yes."

"You would really do it, wouldn't you?"

"It's what I do."

"Do it then?" Xavier grabbed the barrel of my gun and shifted it up to point at his heart. "What's worse a monster who knows what he is or one that pretends to be otherwise? You Van Helsings have a god complex like no other and forget you are just as bad as the rest of us."

He pushed against the barrel until it had to be biting into his flesh, while he whispered, "There's a reason you're the ones the monsters fear."

Check it out on your favorite bookstore!

About the Author

Erin Bedford is an otaku, recovering coffee addict, and Legend of Zelda fanatic. Her brain is so full of stories that need to be told that she must get them out or explode into a million screaming chibis. Obsessed with fairy tales and bad boys, she hasn't found a story she can't twist to match her deviant mind full of innuendos, snarky humor, and dream guys.

On the outside, she's a work from home mom and bookbinger. One the inside, she's a thirteen-year-old boy screaming to get out and tell you the pervy joke they found online. As an ex-computer programmer, she dreams of one day combining her love for writing and college credits to make the ultimate video game!

Until then, when she's not writing, Erin is devouring as many books as possible on her quest to have the biggest book gut of all time. She's written over thirty books, ranging from paranormal romance, urban fantasy, and even scifi romance.

Come chat me up!
www.erinbedford.com
Facebook.com/erinrbedford
twitter.com/erin_bedford
Don't forget to follow me on Goodreads, Pinterest, Instagram, and YouTube!

www.ingramcontent.com/pod-product-compliance
Lightning Source LLC
Chambersburg PA
CBHW070924190726
48292CB00004B/1099